Southern Comfort

Joyce Finch Brown

PublishAmerica
Baltimore

First printing

PublishAmerica has allowed this work to remain exactly as the author intended, verbatim, without editorial input.

ISBN: 1-60703-516-2
PUBLISHED BY PUBLISHAMERICA, LLLP
www.publishamerica.com
Baltimore

Printed in the United States of America

This book is dedicated to Joe and Lois who made me possible, to my loving grandparents, aunts, uncles, brother and sister who gave me so many rich stories to share and to Michael, Stephen, Lorna, Savannah, Baby Paul, Anthony and Bill who continually bring me joy, love and **Southern Comfort.**

Thank you to April Mansfield from June Bug Photography for the pictures of myself included in the promotion of this book.

Southern Comfort... From My Heart to Your Heart... Enjoy!

I am as **Southern** as I think anyone can be and not have a double first name. I do have several last names thanks to being married more than once and when I link all of them together it is quite a mouthful. In the South having a double name is considered "normal". Billy Bob, Bobby Joe, Sulla Belle, Lorna Lou, Jimmie Kay, Monte Clair, Hattie Mae...you get the picture. The Jimmie Kay is the female version of her daddy's name, he is known as Big Jimmy, and Monte Clair was named after her granddaddy, Monte. Of course when you say their names you always use both of the names, never just Jimmie or Monte. I had an Aunt Pete and I never knew what her real/legal name actually was and even my mother doesn't know the answer to that one. I have an Aunt Billie Jean who is my mother's only sibling. Her dad was not a William or a Bill or even a Gene, so I have no idea why she was named Billie Jean. I had another Aunt who legally changed her name from Tisha to Gertrude. Yes, I know it is hard to believe that she paid money to do that but she loved the name Gertrude and wanted it for her very own. Her younger brother always called her Tisha when he was with her and that would make her mad at him and make him laugh when she got mad!

Everyone in my age group remembers Lady Bird Johnson as a truly grand and unique first lady. She was this country's first Lady Bird as first lady and yes, I know that she was from Texas but anyone named Lady Bird has to have a relative somewhere in the South.

In our family if one of your parents or grandparents called you by both of your names, or heaven forbid by all 3 of your names, you knew you were in deep, deep trouble. My brother is a Joe Wayne Clark, Jr. so when he was called by all 3 names plus the Junior he was in serious trouble and we all knew it. Back then as a kid he was Joey so when our mom yelled " Joey Wayne Clark, Jr., you come here this minute" all of us tried to hide!

My maternal grandmother had 2 daughters, Lois and Billie Jean. My name is Joyce and my sister's name is Becki so more than once our grandmother would call us Lois and Billie by mistake, or as she put it, she was just calling the roll until she got to the right name. My mother claims that my name is a combination of Joe and Lois, my parent's names. I think that is just sweet enough that I like to claim it is true. I am the only Joyce in our family and if you say their 2 names quickly it does sound like Joyce. So I guess I can almost qualify as having a double name, what do you think?

I do not see the South changing our naming system anytime soon. Our system has worked very well in the past and I hope it remains just as it is with all of its oddities in the future. We also have a tradition of tacking on *sweet names* like sugar, honey, and sweetie when speaking to a loved one or even to just a friend. With all of the ugly words being spoken every day it is a pleasure to hear someone refer to someone else as "sweetie". They are not being sexist...they are just being gentle and kind.

I was born in a small town in Arkansas named Magnolia. That is one set of Southern roots to start my life. I have spent most of my life in Arkansas and think of this state as home. I wear shoes when necessary but most Southern ladies prefer bare feet, flip flops or fancy sandals. We enjoy our toes and can be very expressive with our feet. Very rarely do you see a Southern lady who does not have her toe nails painted. Nail polish is an accessory we consider fundamental to every Southern lady's feet.

I enjoy living where things are just a wee-bit slower and more laid back. Our summers are hot, our mosquitoes (skeeters) are big and hungry, our ribs are cooked on a slow wood-burning grill and covered with home made BBQ sauce, slaw comes with the BBQ pork sandwich, the internet is still being explored and enjoyed on a daily basis, pick-up trucks are normal types of transportation but so are Cadillac's, and everyone in your community knows your business. The front porch swing may be a thing of the past thanks to air-conditioning but the gossip still flows from house to house. It is unnatural to shut yourself off and not know your neighbors business. What if they needed your help? How would you know if you weren't politely nosey?

I have raised 2 fine young men and am very proud of both of them. They are as different as night and day but the same in all things that are important. They were born 10 years apart so I raised 2 "only child" kids. One is a farmer here in Arkansas and the other is a store executive in Florida. My farmer son has a wife, a little girl and another baby due Christmas Day. My store executive son and his life's partner are not legally married because we do not allow gay couples to marry. I can still remember trying to explain gay to my grandmother. I am not sure that she ever got it but that did not really matter. Both of my sons are loved for who they are, not what they are. It is an enjoyable family gathering when all of us are together. My granddaughter loves her Uncles and they are in charge of her cultural "up-bringing". They will be the Uncles who take her to Europe when she is old enough. I do not think you could pay my other son to get on a plane for that many hours unless he was the pilot.

We all have dreams that we can escape to in our heads when we are seeking relief from the daily pressures of life. I can close my eyes and see myself driving down a beautiful country road in my Nancy Drew inspired bright blue roadster convertible, listening to the Beach Boys sing one of their hit songs from the 70's on my fabulous Bose sound system, enjoying the sunshine on a glorious spring day which has temperatures in the mid-70's, and feeling totally at peace with my life and surroundings. Of course, I may never own that roadster or by the time I can afford to buy a small convertible the enter and exit part of ownership will be "off limits" because I will no longer be able to bend my knees enough to allow me to actually sit in it! Until that day comes I will continue to hold on to my dream and let it continue to bring me **Southern Comfort** just thinking about how wonderful it will be.

We can find true **Southern Comfort** in our memories of family gatherings, in familiar smells when we enter the kitchen, from hearing our children squeal with delight as they run thru the lawn sprinkler or from just watching an elderly couple holding hands as they call each other honey or sweet heart. You draw comfort from the familiar and the things that your heart holds dear. It can be another person, it can be a homemade quilt, it can be using your grandmother's recipe for pineapple upside down cake and serving that cake to your family, all of these things can bring you comfort.

Now turn the page and enjoy reading about what brings **Southern Comfort** to my loved ones and to me. One of our stories may ignite a memory for you that will bring a smile to your heart and laughter to your lips.

WANTED TO PURCHASE:
(1) SLIGHTLY USED ROADSTER CONVERTIBLE!
GOOD SOUND SYSTEM A MUST!
Easy exit and entry a plus!
PLEASE CONTACT ME AND DISCUSS TERMS.
www.dreamscancometrue.dotdot

Southern Comfort... The Older Generation

In the South we value our elderly so it was natural for mother to move in with me when she was retired and no longer wanted to live alone. It is a challenge having the 2 of us living together under one roof but so far we have managed to keep our relationship in the **Southern Comfort** love zone. Actually sometimes it is fun to spar with her verbally and win an argument. She does winter in Florida with my oldest son so she is officially a "snow bird". Yes, Michael has earned his angel wings already and he and my son-in-law are very patient, loving and considerate to her when she is with them.

Nursing homes for our elderly are always a last resort, which means the family has finally agreed that the need for professional care outweighs the need to keep the family member at home. We do have Senior Citizen communities but most families prefer to add a room or make room for their aging relative and keep them where they are fed with daily love.

I would have missed so many opportunities for love if my grandmother hadn't lived with me off and on in her later years. She had so much to share, wonderful stories to tell, and always had such a witty way of putting things in perspective, that she was a joy to be around. I always knew that I could turn to her when I needed **Southern Comfort**. When she told us stories about her life as a young person it seemed like another world because so many changes have taken place in the past 100 years. If the next 100 years are as productive as the past have been we will all live like George Jetson. She grew up without running water or indoor plumbing, electricity was limited, cars had just been invented and not everyone could afford one, telephones were few and far between and if you were lucky enough to have one you were on a party line.

For those of you who do not know what that means...a party line was a phone line shared by more than one family. Each line had a code of the number of rings to let you know if the call was for your number. The polite version of party line rules is you only pick up the receiver if the number of rings is yours. Otherwise when you pick up the receiver you are now eavesdropping on someone's conversation.

I actually shared a line years ago with 2 other families and one of the ladies would pick up and listen in on my conversation. She would even chime in and make comments! Sometimes my mother would just make things up to get the lady interested in our conversation. We had our own soap opera dialogue just for her listening pleasure.

I am quickly approaching the Senior category myself which is a shock to me but I can't deny what the birth certificate says. Actually that may not be entirely true...My paternal grandmother, in her effort to stay young, decided that a couple of her years could just have a little *face lift* and get counted twice! She was part of the generation who were born at home so an official birth certificate signed by a delivery doctor was not possible. The family bible journal of birthdays was the standard used to establish age but the family bible had been lost years before it was needed to prove her real age. My aunt had several months of numerous trips to the social security office to establish her mother's real age when it was time to register her for social security benefits and Medicare.

I am in my last year of the glorious 50's time-cycle in life and have been blessed with very few wrinkles. I contribute this to Southern plumping. My family has always had round, chubby cheeks and more than one chin. This natural fullness discourages wrinkles at any age. If a wrinkle starts I eat another plate of chocolate gravy and biscuits and fill that pesky wrinkle up with natural plumping before it gets a chance to really settle in for good. Southern women knew about chocolate gravy long before anyone thought of using botox to stop wrinkles. It is cheaper, less painful and does not require medical assistance or a needle...and it is all natural!

My mother does not look her age either thanks to Lady Clairol and a few make-up tricks. She still has a lively mind and most of the time can be quite entertaining. She provides interesting stories for my children and she is always good for a dinner out, early bird special preferred when possible. She can really turn the Southern charm on when she is with a good-looking young man. It gives you a glimpse of what she must have been like when she was young and dating. It gives you **Southern Comfort** to know that no matter how old you get a true Southern Belle can still charm the men!

"I'm sorry...but the number you are calling is still busy. Please try again in a few months and hopefully the line will be clear by then."

Southern Comfort...
Drama

Have I mentioned that most Southern women are born to be drama queens? It is in our gene pool probably from all of the hot sauce our daddy's ate before we were conceived. All of us start as a little princess and work our way up to full queen status. You have to start very young and polish this skill. My granddaughter Savannah, at the age of 2, has already learned the fine art of drama. When she does not get her way, she dissolves into tears, collapses on the floor and sobs. It doesn't seem to achieve the result that she would like since both of her parents seem to be immune to her drama sobs. Hurt sobs are different but drama is drama and her parents have already learned to read her well.

Southern ladies also learn to accessorize almost from birth. It is a form of drama when done correctly. Plain is not something that a Southern

Belle can enjoy. Most Southern ladies start to expand this talent of choosing the correct accessories for every outfit at an early age. Usually by the time the young woman is a teenager she has developed this talent into an art form. My granddaughter has already started showing her above average skill in this area. When she agreed to give back a toy in the department store in exchange for a new part of glittery sandals I realized that she is going to be a true Southern Belle. What a proud moment that was for her grandmother!

She recently attended a birthday party for a cousin who is only 3 months younger than she is. The birthday party favors were "dress up" pretties for the little girls. We acknowledge this need for accessories from the time they are very small and do what we can as adults to encourage this art form. The little girls received 2 little party bags filled with young girl jewelry...rings, bracelets, necklaces, movie star sunglasses and to complete the look...a red boa was the ribbon to tie the 2 party bags together.

If those little girls weren't a sight when they got all dolled up??! They squealed, and laughed, and pranced around the room in all of their new finery. Each had a little different twist to the way they put it all together, which indicates they each have a fine sense of their own style even at this early stage of development!

Savannah's great-grandmother lives next door and Savannah is a frequent visitor to her Ma Maw Dean's house. One Saturday morning she was invited to breakfast next door and she didn't need any help on choosing her wardrobe. She selected a new diaper; a bright orange tee shirt with green alligators on it proclaiming the Naples Florida Zoo is a wonderful place to visit, and her clear jellies sandals. Outfit complete...nope. She and her mother got to the door and she remembered she needed her bracelets. Several brightly colored bangle bracelets had to be worn on each arm. Outfit complete...wrong again. She needed a hat. Her hat of choice was her Russian inspired red furry hat. It was July but a pretty hat really knows no season. Now she was ready to go but then she realized there was just one more thing she had to have...her backpack to use as a purse. You can imagine the surprise on her great-grandmother's face when she opened the kitchen door and there stood her great-granddaughter in all of her glory from head to toe decked out in her finest. They were so impressed with her choices that her cousin Shyann took more than one picture of her in this specially chosen outfit. She not only gave everyone a reason to smile she gave her great-grandmother **Southern Comfort** knowing the love of accessories would continue with the next generation.

"Momma, How Much Jewelry Is Too Much Jewelry? Are 5 Bracelets Too Many?"

Southern Comfort...
2 Up and 1 Down

My dad was 1 of 10 children, which was not unusual for his generation. He was one of what I refer to as the Original 10 when I do my monthly family newsletter. The Original 10 had 33 children of which I am #5. We are a big, robust, diverse family. My dad and his older brother, who was only 25 months older, were so much alike in so many ways that you always had fun with them.

I am the oldest of 3 children and my dad died when I was 16. He had a kidney transplant and the donor was his youngest brother who is only 5 years older than I am. When the need for a kidney was revealed to the family every single one of his siblings and his mother came for testing. That shows true **Southern Comfort** to not even hesitate when a brother needs you. Kidney transplants were still in the experimental stage and daddy only lived for 5 short months before a blood clot killed him. For my uncle to agree to be the donor, and he was only 21 years old with a long life ahead of him, shows the true meaning of brotherly love.

When my dad and 6 of his siblings were growing up, the country was just barely coming out of the depression years. Being depressed in Mississippi wasn't anything new to the people who lived there. Hard times were expected because that was the way life had always been. They might not have much money but they had other things that were more important. How many of you have slept 3 to a double bed? Do you know what 2 up and 1 down means? One of the ways they kept warm in the winter was to sleep 3 to a bed. When they were still small they could all 3 fit sideways in a double bed. As they got longer they had to adjust and sleep in the up & down position from the foot of the bed to the headboard. They would sleep with 2 of them laying their head down on pillows at the top/ headboard of the bed and the other one would put his pillow between them at the foot of the bed. This way they had 2 up at the head of the bed and 1 down at the foot of the bed and they would rotate who was up and who was down. Either way you slept you had someone's feet in your face when you woke up.

Everyone had to promise to not kick a brother in his sleep or there would be boys with black eyes the next morning. My dad wore socks to bed every night until he joined the Army! For my dad and his brothers this sleeping arrangement was normal and your brother was not just your brother, he was your friend for life.

Their home had fireplaces & plenty of wood to burn in the main rooms to keep them warm, always an abundance of good home grown food so no need to worry about going to bed hungry, clean clothes, shoes in the winter time, and enough love to make them feel special and safe. **Southern Comfort** to them was a brother or a sister you could play with, talk to and your best friend when it was time to share a piece of hot cornbread and glass of cold milk after you had finished your chores.

Southern Comfort is truly defined by family ties. That loving bond is always there when you need it the most. Sometimes when I see a homeless person begging for money I can't help but wonder where their family is? I want to ask them "Where is your mother and your daddy? Do you have a brother or sister? Don't you have family somewhere that will take you in and take care of you?" I grew up knowing that if one family member couldn't be there that another would step up and take their place. Family was big and the bond was strong. I doubt if many adults today grew up sleeping 2 up and 1 down in the bed. Maybe waking up every morning to see your brother's bare feet in your face made that generation appreciate things more. They at least appreciated the pure joy of having a bed to sleep on each night even if it meant sharing it. **Southern Comfort** to them was a bed...pure and simple...and someone to keep your backside warm when Old Man Winter was knocking on your door.

"Tonight's forecast is for snow, sleet and lows in the 20's! It's time to add an extra blanket and put on some socks!"

Southern Comfort...
Namesakes

Earlier I touched briefly on the need to use double names and to make a female version of a male name. Southern families believe that the past is important and you are always linked to your family. We celebrate our past by having our children become namesakes of previous family members. My youngest son is a Jr. and no matter whom he meets they automatically ask, "Aren't you Steve's son?" Of course his dad is Big Steve and he is Little Stephen to his grandmother. To everyone except his grandmother he is Stephen and his dad is Steve. I do not think anyone else has ever called him "little"! Little Stephen is 6'5", 280 lbs. of little and out grew his daddy many years ago. I bought him a personalized license plate for his first pick up truck and that made him laugh. He told me that was just a waste of good money to pay for it to be personalized since everyone already knew it was his truck. I explained that maybe he would go someplace where everybody did not know him and his answer was "not likely".

We have a few families who believe in naming all of their children with the same first initial. That makes the family have Jimmy, Janie, Jamie, Jennie, Jacob and Johnny...you get the picture. I also know families who have given all of their children the same middle name which can be quite a challenge trying to link a pretty first name to the pre-chosen middle name. All of the little girls will have Anne as a middle name and all of the little boys will have William as their middle name. It is a way of keeping continuity and linking all of the children together by more than just their last name.

Most young women of the South do not keep their maiden name when they marry but they no longer become only known as Mrs. James Smith which is what most of the older generations did. Very few of the previous generations of Southern women established their own separate identities. Most of my aunts are still signing all of their checks as Mrs. James Smith...never just Jane Smith. The thought of not being Mrs. James Smith never even came into their heads. It simply was not "done".

We have special links sometimes from brother-to-sister or cousin-to-cousin. My brother was my birthday present from my 6th birthday. This was light years before you could plan a pregnancy so for him to be born on my birthday was something to celebrate. The only thing with that celebration was, it was not a unique experience to our family. My maternal grandmother Emma and her baby brother Clyde were born exactly 6 years apart, too.

My granddaughter and her cousin Kari share the same birthday and they also share the same strawberry shaped birthmark in the exact same place on their legs. And to make it even more special Kari is a teenager and her mother is Savannah's aunt. So the birthmark "skipped" Savannah's mother but then re-entered the family when Savannah was born. Try topping that one!

In the South the name given to a baby is considered one of the most important responsibilities a parent has and we take pride in naming our children. We honor the past by continuing names from one generation to another. It gives us comfort to know that the name will go forward with the next generation and hopefully into the one after that. Most of the time when someone knows the present Paul Houston they knew the previous Paul Houston and tell you how wonderful the previous Paul Houston was. They will tell you that the person you are named after was a wonderful person and would be very proud of you. It gave your parent's comfort to name you after a loved one because it means that person is still alive in a small way. You are now connected to their past and that is now a part of your past. We take **Southern Comfort** in acknowledging that we look like another relative. Kind of keeps the gene pool right out in the open!

From Social Section of Local Newspaper: Smith family reunion held this past weekend. I was included as a special guest. I never saw so many red headed children and freckles in one place. You could really see the family resemblance. No doubt that they were all related!

Southern Comfort...
Southern Cooking

The heart of a Southern home is the kitchen. It has to be big enough to handle all of the family when they decide to gather in it to see "what's cooking". You very rarely, if ever, see a galley kitchen in a Southern home. We need plenty of counter top space and lots of elbowroom and big pantries and lots of cabinet space.

I do not know what comfort food is in the North but I do know what it is in the South. It almost always includes mashed potatoes and home made sweet milk gravy. We use buttermilk to make our biscuits, to coat our fried chicken before we coat it again with seasoned flour, to make our cornbread and to make our cakes from scratch. (Made from scratch means not out of a box!)

Buttermilk helps to calm your stomach if you are feeling a little bit queasy. If you cook with it that should eliminate the need for TUMS later. When you are feeling down or out-of-sorts have yourself some Southern fried chicken that was cooked in the only type of skillet to use to have perfect fried chicken. That skillet is a large iron skillet. Every Southern kitchen has at least one large iron skillet. Most homes have a minimum of 2 since you also need one to make cornbread. I have a recipe handed down to me from my grandmother for an iron skillet version of upside down pineapple cake.

My daughter-in-law made Sweet Water Rolls to take to a 4th of July party. Everyone kept asking if they were *home made* and of course she made them from scratch. The guests were very impressed and she did not have a single roll to bring back home. Actually her husband didn't even get one since he was at the tail end of the serving line. Home made is worth the effort and is very appreciated and evidently very impressive. She received complement after complement

The beverage of choice in almost all Southern kitchens is iced tea. It is sweet iced tea since no Southern kitchen would serve it any other and it is cold in the "ice box" when you need it. Yes, we have moved on to refrigerators but "ice box" sticks in your head and it is hard to get out.

You may notice that I mentioned sweet milk earlier. That's because I grew up with sweet milk and sour milk. The sweet milk is what the rest of the world calls milk (2%/ low fat/ whole milk) and sour milk is buttermilk. Buttermilk can have a sour taste and odd smell if it is really good buttermilk. It needs to have a little kick to it!

A hot piece of Southern fried chicken, a bowl of mashed potatoes and gravy, and a tall glass of sweet iced tea will remove the grump from just about anyone. If that doesn't mellow you out then you need to go to the Doctor for professional help because something is definitely *"not right"* with you. This is **Southern Comfort** at its' best!

"I was feeling kind of tuckered out but after that good meal I'm ready to go! Thanks momma!"

Southern Comfort...
Southern Daddies

Every time a little Southern girl is born her daddy's aging process automatically speeds up. His hair is now on high speed recolor to gray and will be almost white from worry by the time his little girl goes out on her first date. If he is on slow speed it won't start to recede and /or fall out until after the first date but the process has begun. That little girl is his little darlin from the minute he lays eyes on her. There is a special bond between her and her daddy that will never be broken. She can always come to him when her little heart is broken, when the boy she is madly in love with does not feel the same way or when she wrecks her mother's car. Her daddy will give her his shoulder to cry on and comfort her. He also will expect her to put her cowgirl boots on and climb up on the tractor and give him some help when he needs her. She has been riding on tractors since she was in diapers and can run one as good as any boy ever could. Of course she has to get ready which involves the right pair of jeans, some lip gloss, sunglasses, a cute ball cap to pull her pony tail thru, and a large beverage to keep her from getting thirsty. Depending on her mood that morning, one of her daddy's work shirts may be confiscated for a good cause and become part of her work wardrobe.

She can drive a tractor all day, come in and take a bubble bath, put her high heeled sandals on her manicured feet, pile her hair up and head on out the door for a night on the town. She may have dirt in the morning and perfume at night but she is truly a Southern girl. That fragile little 5 foot nothing can hold her own when she has to and doesn't back down no matter how big the problem may be. If she can not talk her way out of it she can always call her daddy for back up.

A Southern girl knows no matter how old she gets she can always count on her daddy. He fell madly in love with her the first time he laid eyes on her and she will always be his little girl even when she is 60 and he is 85. She knows that she can always come to her daddy when she needs some **Southern Comfort**.

When her daddy is not available she can turn to her granddaddy for love and understanding. When she and her daddy don't quite see eye-to-eye the man she can count on to be in her corner and help make her daddy *"see the light"* is her sweet, loving granddaddy. It is hard to believe the stories she can hear from time to time about how wild that sweet, gray haired, loving, calm granddaddy was in his "miss-spent youth". The aging process has mellowed him to the point that whatever his little darlin needs is what she should have...within reason. Of course, his point of reason and her daddy's point of reason may not even be within a mile of each other. It truly gives her grandmother **Southern Comfort** to just watch and see how the 2 men in her granddaughter's love circle work things out.

"Isn't she the most precious thing you ever saw? And so good to her daddy!"

Southern Comfort... True Friends

This past Father's day a close friend of my daughter-in-law's was killed in a car accident. The young woman was only 30 years young and the mother of two little girls aged 9 and 11. The 9 yr old little girl was with her mother but was asleep in the front seat and had her seat belt on for protection. Their vehicle was rear-ended and the mother was killed instantly. The miracle is the little girl survived with bruises. Now the husband is left to raise two little girls by himself...only he is not by himself. They have lived in a small town all of their lives and therefore everyone knows them and in this case will give them comfort and help when needed. The afternoon of the tragedy my daughter-in-law Lorna and a couple of other ladies that knew the young woman went to her house and cleaned it...even cleaned out the refrigerator of old food. They automatically knew that they were needed and didn't think twice about going to *"put things right"* for their friend's family.

In the South when someone is badly hurt or has a death in the family Southern woman start cooking and baking. We take the family whatever we can put together in a hurry and then do better with the next trip. To go to the home of someone and clean it to *"make it right"* for the husband and children was as natural to these young women as putting on your Sunday best to attend church. You just get your apron on and put it in high gear and start cleaning.

I know from first hand experience that when a new baby is born neighbors and relatives will bring a casserole over as a welcome home gift. I had that happen many, many years ago. It meant more than flowers ever would because it was one less thing I had to do to take care of my family.

These women have made a pact with each other that when another one dies the other 2 will step up to the plate and make sure the dearly departed has her make up on and that it is applied correctly. They have agreed to just *suck it up* and do whatever they have to do so their friend won't be seen at her funeral without her make-up properly applied and looking pretty. That might sound odd to some of you but I have an Aunt who never let her husband see her without her lipstick on and her hair combed and brushed. She was brought up with the understanding a lady never left her bedroom with bedroom hair and after a certain age she should have her lipstick on too.

Southern Comfort is given from the heart and usually without much thought. You just automatically do it... It is the right thing to do. These young women all have big **Southern Comfort** hearts. They don't think about doing it...they just do it. It is a natural, built-in instinct. My wish for all of you is that you have **Southern Comfort** friends and family. You never know when you need them but it is always good to know that they are there if you do.

"Welcome home from the hospital. Here's a hot pot roast, a cold salad, and a right-out-of-the-oven chocolate cake for your family to have for dinner tonight. I'll come back tomorrow and bring more."

Southern Comfort...
Bubba's Good Old Boys

To clear up the confusion between Red Neck and Bubba is pretty complicated and hard to explain in words on paper. You really need to be Southern to completely get the difference but I'll try and explain it.

Good Old Boys (normally pronounced without the D in Old) are the friends a Southern man has developed over most of his life. They are the friends (Bubba's) that you can call at 2AM when you've managed to drive your truck into a ditch because you were too tired to still be up or you were tired and had maybe one too many beers before you headed down that gravel road to your driveway. They are the daddy's of other young "Bubba's in Training" who spot a young Bubba in trouble and help the young one out without telling his daddy what happened. They at least give the young Bubba a chance to tell his daddy first with a time limit set at the trouble spot for this discussion to take place. After that the older Bubba will talk to the young Bubba's daddy just to make sure he knows that his son needs a little guidance counseling. They have their own code of ethics and can be counted on to come to the aid of another Bubba without hesitation. If there is a storm and you can not get home to your family they are the men you call to make sure someone gets over there to protect your family from harm.

They are a modern Southern version of the Knights of old. They believe in family, they believe women are to be respected, and they can be trusted to be there when you really need a friend and to give **Southern Comfort** if needed.

A Bubba can be a red neck but it is not required. A Red Neck has his own code of honor that may or may not necessarily be the same as the Bubba code. You can be one without being the other.

The Bubba men are the Good Old Boys of the community who do good acts of kindness and community work without being asked. They just follow their hearts and know what needs to be done. They may look big and tough but they all have hearts as big as their boots.

"Do you think we ought to check on Bob's family while he's away? It wouldn't hurt and if they need anything we'll take care of it while we're there."

Southern Comfort...
Man's Best Friend

Almost every Southern family has a 4-legged best friend and 99% of those are dogs. We're not really Cat people if you know what I mean. It is almost impossible to train a cat to jump up into the back of the pick up truck bed and go with you when you leave to go to work on the farm. Most farms that have a barn will have what we call "working cats" that are responsible for keeping the mice out of the barn and the house but generally they are not traveling companions.

Some of our dogs have unusual names like Dog but most of them are called Old Blue, Duke, Beau, Big Red, Molly, Sally, Dandy. We try and keep the names simple so when you have to yell for the dog it doesn't come out sounding silly (pedigree names are usually long and complicated). Every "young Bubba in training" needs his own dog for loving, discipline and to learn responsibility. My farmer son had a dog that absolutely loved to ride in the truck and she would sleep in the bed of the truck so she would be there first thing when my son left out the next morning. He would come out of the house and there she would be waiting, standing up in the truck bed, leaning over the cab roof, smiling and wagging her tail hello. It is hard not to smile even if you are half asleep when you are met with such love and devotion.

I had a neighbor who took the love of animals a little to the extreme. He had his own petting zoo built behind his house. He raised a fainting lama (yes, they really do faint), miniature potbelly pigs, a Shetland pony, and birds of all descriptions including Leroy the Peacock. Leroy enjoyed flying up to the peak of the roof on my 2 story home and filling the air with his screeching. His owner had him trained to follow him around and obey simple commands. I did not really appreciate the beauty of Leroy after he left me a few "presents" on my black roof, if you know what I mean?

We have conversations with our animals and I swear to you they do know what we are saying and give us the proper respect when we are feeling down and/ or blue. They will come and give you **Southern**

Comfort when you need it. They just know that what you need is a extra little-bit of sugar that morning and they give your face an extra wash...as in a few good licks will make us both feel better. Now that is truly **Southern Comfort**.

"HEY, MOLLY! Are you ready for another day on the farm, girl?"

Southern Comfort...
Sunday Church Suppers and
Ice Cream Socials

Sunday Night Church Suppers were something to look forward to when I was a youngster and we had one a month at our church. This was the time for each woman in the congregation to show off one of her prize-winning recipes. You never went home hungry after attending one of these. The competition was keen and the women of the church never brought anything but their best. Each of the Corning Ware casserole dishes had the owners name clearly attached to it for clean up purposes but we all knew it was to let you know who made each dish. One lady always brought just one chocolate pie...never two. We would fight over who would get a piece and that is just the way she liked it. She could always leave with an empty pie plate and brag to everyone how quickly her pie *"disappeared"*.

Some of the ladies didn't have family to cook for anymore and this was the one time of the month that they could enjoy cooking and have their recipes truly appreciated. It gave them **Southern Comfort** for a member of the congregation to ask them to make a certain dish. It meant that they were still special and loved and remembered. I think it was the remembered part that gave them the most **Southern Comfort**.

Homemade ice cream is a treat that everyone in the South enjoys. All of us have our own "secret" recipe for that special version that is uniquely ours. My Aunt Tava has a recipe that she has graciously shared with the rest of our family for fresh peach ice cream. It has enough extra ingredients in it to make everyone like it even if they aren't that fond of peaches. The recipe calls for a tablespoon of vanilla followed up with a ½ tablespoon of almond extract.

We have electric ice cream freezers now but I grew up helping to hand crank the original, which was a metal can placed down inside a small wooden barrel-like container. Cranking it inside the house, where it was air-conditioned, just was not something that anyone would allow you to do, so that meant finding a shady place outside in the heat and cranking, and cranking, and cranking some more. Once you got the rock salt, water and ice combination just right you started to see some progress in the thickening process inside the metal canister. When you finished you had to "pack it down" with more ice and a big heavy towel on top for weight and let it continue to freeze. The end result was always worth all of the work.

Most Southern churches plan at least one ice cream social each summer. All of the women bring their best recipes and the husbands are in charge of the freezing process. Everyone goes home with full bellies and are already talking about what recipe they will fix for the next one. The competition can be fierce but always friendly for the Best Ice Cream of the social.

It gives a hostess **Southern Comfort** to only have a cup or 2 of ice cream left over and to send her guests home *full as a tick* and "wishing that they could have just one more bowl" is one of the biggest compliments she can ever get. If you have anything left over it is always special enough to go in the freezer and be eaten at a later date. This rarely happens...but when it does finding a small container of home made ice cream in the freezer a few weeks later is always appreciated by the "Sherlock" who was lucky enough to discover it!

"Nothing beats homemade ice cream! And 2 scoops are always better than just one!!"

Southern Comfort... Small Town Stores

Another plus to living in a small Southern town is you can call the local drugstore and order a BLT to go with you prescription and pick up a good sandwich and beverage the same time you pick up your new medication. You can also run a "tab" for the month and pay the store the end of the month. This is very handy when your teenage child is hungry and doesn't have any money with them. "Just charge it to my daddy" usually takes care of the problem.

Charging fuel and tires to the husband's account is not just something that is seen on TV shows or in the movies. The movie "The Notebook" shows the wife pulling up at the local service station/ small grocery store and asking to get some cash instead of gasoline and put it on her husband's account. She and another woman work it out and she leaves with the cash that she wanted. Trust me...it happens everyday in the South in small towns. This system of banking was our first **ATM** before the banks ever even thought of a drive up money withdrawal machine!

I was married to a farmer in a small town and occasionally the bank would call to tell me that the personal account was going to be over drawn with what had been presented for payment. That meant I had to find my husband for him to move operating money out of one account into his personal account. That is what we call friendly banking service in the **South**. Today I am told some banks actually charge the customer to speak to a *live person*!

When I was a youngster we had a family owned pharmacy run by Big Jimmy and his son Little Jimmy. The Jimmy's had the sliding scale of payment back then. If a down-on-his-luck daddy needed cough syrup for his child, Big Jimmy would either give it to him for free or give it to him at a big discounted price. Sometimes if one of the Bubba's knew about the situation they would take care of it by simply telling Big Jimmy to put it on their account. This was done politely so that the man needing a little extra help wouldn't feel like he was a charity case. The Bubba's have a communication system and always do what needs to be done quietly. I personally think the CIA could learn a thing or two from them. A Bubba does not want attention for doing a good deed. Bubba's believe in quiet dignity and a man's business is his own business. **Southern Comfort** means lending a helping hand without expecting a "pat on the back."

"Bob, just put that on my husband's account. He'll be along soon to pay for it. And while you're at it fill up John's pick up, too. I know he can use a little help right now with his kids being sick. My husband won't mind if we add a little more to my ticket."

Southern Comfort...
Neighborhood Watch

Everyone knows the *"unusual"* members of the community and watches out for them...literally. If you see one of them, who sometimes goes a little slower than the speed limit because they are afraid to speed up, you just adjust your speed to accommodate them. You give them plenty of room when they are pulling into the parking lot at the local grocery. If they decide to park at an unusual angle you do not get alarmed. At least they got the car parked so no harm/ no foul. We recognized handicapped parking many, many years before it became official enough to have special parking places allocated.

When you meet one of the *"unusual"* members driving on a busy street you do your very best defensive driving and everyone stays safe. They never venture out at night or in bad weather and just need to go to the grocery and the drug store a few times a month so the police do not seem too alarmed. There are always plenty of neighbors to watch out for them and make sure nobody gets hurt. If they forget to turn the car off when they get back home a neighbor will eventually come over and shut if off and deliver the keys. We try and treat everyone with respect and love. We had *Neighborhood Watch* established many years before it became a national thing to do. We just called it watching out for our neighbors who might need a little extra **Southern Comfort** from time to time.

I see signs now in larger cities designating different stores, restaurants, etc. as "safe places" for children to come to if they need help. Growing up in a small town in the South, I had safe places in so many places that I probably couldn't have told you where all of them were. I had aunts and uncles, 2 sets of grandparents, and family friends all over that town. I could easily ride my bicycle to any one of them and would know that I was someplace "safe".

My granddaughter is growing up in a small community where she knows "safe" places but she just calls them...Aunt Teresa's house, Ma Maw Dean's house, Uncle George and Aunt Janet's house and Miss Bonnie's Cafe. By now most of the people in her small town know her, and believe me if they ever saw her alone, they would automatically provide her with "safe" whatever was needed. There are definitely negatives in living in such a small community but the pluses are by far so big and powerful that having to do without a few things is well worth it.

To know that she has so many neighbors, family and friends watching over her gives her grandmother **Southern Comfort** and peace of mind.

"If you see Miss Louise pulling into the parking lot move your vehicle as far away from her as possible. She requires a little practice parking before she finally settles on a spot."

Southern Comfort...
Showing Respect

I have grown up with the adults being referred to with respect by calling them Miss Joyce and Mister Bill. To hear a young man refer to an elderly lady with respect makes me smile and it usually makes the elderly ladies face light up. This gives her the opportunity to strike up a conversation with the young man.

If his mother raised him right and taught him how to converse with the older ladies, he will have her smiling and laughing within just a few minutes of greeting her. He should explain if he were only a few years older "how tempted he would be to court her if she were available." That will make her giggle...trust me.

This remark gives her the opportunity to respond back with "what a rascal he is" and the fun really begins. The art of flirting never dies no matter the age of the woman. If she was a flirt at 13 she is still a flirt at 83 and probably has new tricks to try out on the young man, too. Nobody can flirt better than an older Southern lady. By the time she is in her 80's she has perfected it and if they gave out Gold Medals she would have one around her neck! All of it is good, innocent fun and is actually good for her and the young man. She enjoys the attention and he is learning that beauty comes from the inside and never goes away no matter how many years and lines show on the face.

To watch an elderly gentleman take an elderly ladies hand, help her seat herself at the table, and then tell her how lovely she looks will always bring a tear to my eye. The gentle in gentleman is not as present in today's generation as it has been in the past. I think it will eventually come back around and young men will see the benefits from being gentlemen.

The other night my mother and I went out to dinner at a local restaurant in our small community. When we were seated in our booth one of the men at the booth across from us kept smiling at my mother. She made the mistake of smiling back at him so he took that as encouragement. When he and his 2 friends had finished their dinner he stopped by to "chat up" my mother. He patted her on the shoulder, told her what a great meal she was going to have and that it would be even better with a pitcher of beer, winked at her and then told her to have a lovely evening and that he hoped to see her again soon. The look on my mother's face was truly a Polaroid moment. She was so flustered and just kept referring to him as "that old fool"! A little flirting did put the color back in her cheeks...and thank goodness it was beauty shop day so she was looking her best. I teased her and said "mother, you've still got IT!". Her reply back to me was " if I've got IT...I intend to keep IT all to myself!!!"

Every woman, no matter how old or how young, loves to be treated with respect. It will put the sun back in the sky for her and it is such an easy thing to do. Having someone show you respect always puts you at ease and gives you a sense of **Southern Comfort.**

"Did you see the way he was looking at me? He must be 80 if he's a day. The Old Flirt!"

Southern Comfort...
The Sisterhood

Southern sisters may or may not be linked to you by genetics. If you are very, very lucky you will find a Southern sister living next door to you. I have such a friend that I have loved for over 50 years. We started our relationship in ponytails and playing dolls and it has lasted into the later years as we call this time in our lives. We actually looked enough alike as children to tell strangers that we were sisters. One summer we had identical swimsuits to wear to the public swimming pool. Let me tell you...we thought we were truly something with a capital "S". We had an immediate bond of the heart that has carried us thru some really tough times.

The Sisterhood has kicked into high gear for me on more than one occasion. When they ask you to call them if you need something they do not just wait for the call. They *interfere* in your life to bring you conversation, love, comfort, and whatever they know that you need even if you are not emotionally steady enough to realize it yourself at the time.

Young Southern girls are in training to belong to the Sisterhood the minute they start picking out their own clothes to wear. Their first trainer is their mother and she will be their guide for the rest of their lives. They know to trust her and to believe she will only tell them the truth. The attraction to the older Southern sisters starts at an early age. It's almost like the younger girls have magnets attached to their hair barrettes that pull them to the older girls they meet. The younger girls want to be *just like them*. Once they "attach", that link will always be there, so the older girls know their area of responsibility in the Sisterhood has now officially begun. Never lead a little sister into harm is their code of ethics. Sometimes I think they have their own language like twins have and only a true member of the Sisterhood can translate it. These young Southern girls will grow up to be the next generation of loving, caring, intelligent, witty, out spoken, young Southern ladies. They are never too proud to ask for another sister's help or to give help. It's just a natural instinct that gets stronger as they mature into Southern Sisters. It gives me **Southern**

Comfort to know that what is good and true will be carried forward by these wonderful young women of the South.

Rule #1: Always listen to your momma. You may not like what she's saying but she is only trying to protect you!"

Southern Comfort...
Holidays

As you can imagine the biggest holiday in the South is Christmas. We still prefer to use a fresh cut tree even though it is very tempting to buy a pre-lit artificial tree. Nothing puts you in the holiday spirit like coming home to a house that smells of Christmas Tree and I do not mean from a scented candle or spray can. Yes, I agree that real trees are more trouble from beginning to end but I still will go to the Christmas tree market and walk the aisles until I find the exact tree for the year. I have made a few mistakes with my choices. One year I brought the "perfect" tree into the house and the moment it was upright in the tree stand I realized that it had a twisted trunk and wouldn't stay up straight. The solution after many attempts to compensate for this irregularity was to tie the top of the tree to the curtain rod. My children still remember that tree!

My daddy's oldest sister would flock her trees using an attachment on her vacuum cleaner. One year she added some pink coloring to the flocking and had the prettiest pale pink-flocked tree. My daddy took one look at it and told her that was against the Christmas decorating rules and she never used pink again. It really was pretty with nothing but white lights and white bulbs but it definitely wasn't a traditional Christmas look.

Another holiday that is right up there on top of our list is the 4th of July, which according to my granddaddy Clark that was the official date to start eating sweet watermelon. Evidently the melon needs to stay on the vine until them to get that extra *sweet* he so loved. He would have several melons iced down in big tubs on the 4th and I remember eating really good, sweet watermelon on those holidays. This was many, many years before seedless variety was developed. He loved to buy the big round black diamond variety of melon from Mississippi. When he would cut into it you could hear the pop and that let you know it was ripe and ready to eat. He, being the oldest at the celebration, decided he should have the best of the melon and he would eat the heart out of one. That meant the kids all got pieces with seeds and we learned to eat and spit seeds at a very early age. My granddaughter had watermelon at the baby sitters and showed all of the other kids how to spit the seeds. She is only 2 but she draws from a gene pool of "seed spitters" for many generations.

This holiday also meant the uncles would wear Bermuda shorts and some kind of casual shoes to the party. There were some white, white legs showing on those days and some sun burned uncles the next day. The kids would have Kool-Aid with lots of sugar to keep us buzzing around the yard and the adults would have Kool-Beer to keep them from caring how much buzzing the kids did. By the time it was dark enough for the fireworks both generations were ready for bed. That was many years ago but I can still remember the joy of being with all of my family and playing with my cousins. That was definitely **Southern Comfort** for all ages.

"Pass the mosquito repellent! The skeeters are making a meal out of me!!"

Southern Comfort...
Pass the Salt

If you watch old movies regarding the South, Gone with the Wind for instance, you will see the riverboats were actually floating card parties. The Riverboat gambler was depicted wearing a fancy hat, a brocade vest and carrying a silver-tipped cane. He almost always was shown with his trusty derringer pistol up his sleeve to take care of card cheats who had one too many aces.

He was colorful and just a wee bit wicked with a new lady friend in every port up and down the Mississippi. That was then...

Today the big time gambler in the South usually wears a ball cap, blue jeans, and work boots. His transportation is a 4-wheel drive pick-up truck and the only gun he carries is his hunting rifle. His name isn't Rhett Butler. His name is Billy Bob and he is the farmer who risks everything each year on another crop. Farming is in his blood and he is probably a 4th generation farmer. His set of dice at the craps table is a bag of rice seed and acres and acres of farmland to plant and harvest. Las Vegas is just another pretty place to visit.

His adversaries each year are Mother Nature, insects, and the market. When he is lucky enough to defeat all 3 of these and come out a winner it is another great year on the farm. Sometimes if he is very, very lucky it is not just a great year. It is a really great year and he will have what is referred to as "carry over money". That is his *stake* to start next years crop. His belief in farming as a way of life, and his ability to do it well, are what keeps him coming back year after year.

His knowledge of the soil, the crops, the machinery, the logistics of getting everything harvested on time and delivered, the day-to-day management of his crew, the market, the budget, and every other thing he must handle has the stress level of most CEO positions on Wall Street.

The pressure of risking everything every year, which in most cases involves not just his immediate family but extended family as well, is enormous and does produce a side effect known as "pass the salt" that is seen in almost all farmers. To observe this *condition* you need to visit a small town restaurant in a farming area. It is a gathering place for morning coffee and usually for lunch. This small town restaurant always has either one big round table or 2 long tables that are the designated seating areas for the farmers of the community. Think of this as their board room if you will. They gather in the mornings when time is available and talk over the weather and who is doing what on each farm. This can be classified as a gathering of important information to help guide them thru their decisions. When they can meet at lunch time, for a working lunch, the table will fill up with the farmers and usually at least one salesman from the tractor supply or seed supply company. The condiments on the table will include hot sauce, black pepper, Chow Chow (a Southern relish) and table salt. If you observe the distribution of the condiments you realize that the only person at the table using table salt is the salesman. The farmers will all "pass the salt" without using any on their food. The reason for this is the number of years in farming and /or the number of acres, or both, have taken a toll on the farmer's blood pressure.

They may look like they are just ordinary men in blue jeans wearing ball caps but these are the captains of industry for the South. You will never get one of these blue jean farming CEO's to discuss profit and loss with you but you can get them to tell you if they had a good harvest.

The pride in their voice is not boastful. It is there because they have earned the right to feel proud. To take a man of the soil and put him in an office, force him to wear a suit and use a blackberry every day would surely be a slow and painful death for him. They are born to be in the sun, wind, rain, cold or whatever Mother Nature has for them that day. They are not hothouse orchids who need a controlled atmosphere to flourish. They are the wild flowers that you see grow up between rocks and they take whatever is dished out at them.

Southern Comfort for these wonderful farmers is to sit in their pick-up truck at the end of a long and productive day, sip on a cold drink, watch their rice crop waving in the breeze as the sun sets and knowing that they have spent the day doing what they love to do best.

"How are you doing, Stephen? Crop looking good? Nope, just fair to middlin but I'm hoping for the best!"

Southern Comfort...
Recycling

Women of the South joined the recycling movement years before it was the politically and environmentally correct *thing to do*. I can remember my grandmother Emma using the Rainbow Bread wrappers as her twist tie storage bags. Once the bread wrapper was empty she would rinse it out, hang it up to dry and then use it when she had something to "wrap" and put in the refrigerator. My mother-in-law never used a piece of aluminum foil just one time. It could be used over and over again and frequently was. When we finished eating our baked potatoes she would gather all of the pieces of foil, wipe them clean, fold them neatly and put them back in the drawer for the next time she baked potatoes.

When a mayonnaise jar was empty, she would wet the label to soak it enough to peel it off, and then she washed the jar and the lid and added it to her container collection. If all of us would practice this we would hurt the sales of plastic storage containers, which by the way are a bi-product of oil.

At our house dried out bread was soaked in milk and egg and made into bread pudding. Even left over mashed potatoes would find a way of making it back to the dinner table. They would reappear as potato pancakes. All you needed were the left over potatoes, some flour, salt, black pepper, a little bit of mustard and a small amount of chopped onion. Mix all of this together until you can form small thin patties. The patties are then quick fried in hot oil in an iron skillet. When you smelled them cooking you headed for the kitchen so your brother would not eat them all!

Nothing was wasted and the recipes were good enough that you never felt like you were eating "left overs". I don't think my grandmother lived long enough to even hear the word recycle. She was just being frugal and thrifty and was taught to never waste anything as a child growing up during the depression.

Hand-me-down clothes were what all of us had unless you were lucky enough to be the oldest but that had drawbacks. As the oldest you got the new things but you also did not get as many clothes to wear as the younger children. The younger children would get your hand-me-downs plus a few new things.

Sometimes an old dress would be made new again by reworking it and the mother and child would both take pride in the "new" dress. The pretty "almost new" dress showed how much the mother loved the child. The mother took the extra time to make it an original for that child. Those dresses were passed on from generation to generation. I have an aunt who was a wonderful seamstress. Her vision has betrayed her in her later years and she no longer can see well enough to sew anything but in her younger years she was one of the best. She made coats and dresses for her granddaughter, which later were passed down to another granddaughter and now are in the closet of her great-granddaughter. These items are respected and loved and every single one of them is cherished. They are the very best of recycling because of the love factor.

I have 6 or 7 of my grandmother's handmade quilts. Talk about recycling and not wasting anything! This lady used scraps from every garment she made to make the quilts and they were called crazy quilts for a very good reason. They had a little bit of every kind of fabric on them. They were backed with empty cotton bags that once held flour and still had the flour name stamped on them. I do not know what she used for the fill but years later these wonderful quilts are just as strong as they were the day she finished them.

It is fun to pick out pieces of fabric in the quilt and remember what the garment was she wore made from the rest of the fabric. She also made structured quilts like Sun Bonnet Sue, the Dutch Girl, star burst and of course the wedding ring. Every square was made from different fabric and they all coordinated when she *built* the quilt. Her handiwork was exceptional and the love and patience it took to make one of these quilts is inspiring. She took scraps and made them into something really special. The finished quilts provided beauty and warmth in the wintertime and always gave you **Southern Comfort** when you laid your head on your pillow and covered yourself with one of her "love quilts".

"My goodness Lacey, but that sure is a very pretty dress. Thank you, Mam. My Granmere Tava made it just for me."

Southern Comfort...
All Aboard

When a Southern lady decides that it is time to travel she never travels with just a few things and only one piece of luggage. That simply is not something that she can do and still have a good time on the trip. Spur of the moment does not happen very often either since that can cause multiple problems when she arrives at her destination and realizes that she left her very best dancing shoes back at home. We always believe that more is best so we bring everything that we can possibly fit into a few suitcases. As long as we can close the bag and still lift it up onto the scale at the airport it is not too heavy or too full.

I really feel sorry for the security inspectors at the airports when they are unlucky enough to get one of our suitcases. I have a friend who will only travel with brand new, never worn, still has the tags attached to it, underwear. The thought of a stranger holding up her underwear for inspection is more than she thinks she should have to handle. Just the thought of it would spoil her whole vacation! My elderly aunt has her own way of handling the undergarment handler at baggage check-in. She puts all of her "under things" in a big zip lock bag. On the outside of the bag she writes in big bold letters: "*These undergarments have been worn by an 87-year-old woman. Handle at your own risk!*" That should at least make the inspector think twice about opening that plastic bag.

This new rule about how many ounces of liquid, including makeup in your purse or carry-on luggage, goes completely against everything that a Southern woman holds near and dear to her heart. One small bottle of foundation is never enough. We always have to "blend" several to get the exact shade that we want. Trying to explain that to a bald man who has just one big uni-brow is futile. He is holding your make-up bag hostage and threatening to empty the contents into the nearest garbage can. How would a terrorist ever make something threatening out of base coat Covergirl? Trust me...nothing that you can say will persuade him that you are only going to use this bottle of make-up on your face and not as a base for a bomb.

If you have never traveled with the elderly you have missed one of life's most interesting and most of the time entertaining adventures. My mother is now almost 80 so traveling with her is always a trip...even if it's just to the neighborhood grocery store. She loves...make that LOVES...the electric carts at the bigger stores. She always wants the fastest one and has been known to race other carts to a certain package of meat at the meat counter. It is amazing how agile she can be when she spots a package of pork chops that have the "look" she wants. It is almost like watching Dodge-Em cars when you have several elderly customers trying to pass each other in the aisle. It almost qualifies as an Indy Race if you can get enough speed to pass a few of the other competitors.

This past spring my family took a short cruise to the Bahamas. This was my mother's first cruise and her joy in the whole experience was wonderful to watch. The group consisted of my mom, my oldest son Michael, my son-in-law Anthony, his mother Mary Lou, my husband Bill and myself. Each of us had our own special comfort items that we had to bring for the 3-day trip. My son and I each had a case of Diet Coke, my husband had his case of Diet Mountain Dew, my son-in-law had his pillow and small bedside table fan, but my mother topped us all. She had her 4-wheel walker with fold down seat and a large container of her Irish Crème Coffee Creamer. You would have thought we were refugees fleeing the homeland with our comfort items. Anthony's mom, Mary Lou, brought her cold hard cash and credit cards. We referred to her money as cold hard cash because she used the refrigerator as her safe. Her purse was either on her arm or it was "safe" in the refrigerator.

With her and my mother along we had special treatment from all of the ships personnel. My mother had her 4-wheel walker and she was treated with special care and since we were her companions we received the same extra attention. If you have an elderly relative take them with you because trust me the cruise lines all know how to take care of their special passengers. Mother and her steward were on a first name basis within just a few hours of our leaving port.

You should also take someone like her with you if you want to know everything about everybody on the ship. She is Barbara Walters and Geraldo all rolled up in one. She innocently asks the most personal questions of complete strangers and they for some unknown reason answer her back. It is entertaining to just sit back and watch her work her magic.

The love of travel started with me when I was just a small child. I guess with my daddy and most of his brothers and his father all having careers as truck drivers I have traveling DNA. I grew up in a time when you could take trains to almost any city in the United States. My grandmother and I would board a train in Memphis, TN and travel to Fort Worth, TX to visit my aunt. Those were wonderful adventures. You "rented" a pillow, bought a snack, and lay down in the seat. In just a few minutes I would be sound asleep thanks to the swaying motion of the train and the rhythm of the clicking noise on the tracks. I always loved to travel with my grandmother and kept my suitcase packed just in case she needed me to go with her. My granddaddy would drive to Fort Worth sometimes to bring my grandmother back home and he would take me with him for company. I was not much company because the trips were always at night and he would barely get out of town before I was asleep in the back seat. He made this wonderful bed for me and I could hear the hum of the tires on the road and that is all it took. I would wake up hours later and we would be in Fort Worth.

When I got my driver's license that was the

beginning of my years and years of being in the drivers seat. Even as a teenager I would be the designated driver when we took trips. I grew up behind the wheel and never had any fear of driving myself anywhere, anytime or in almost any weather. My daddy was a long distance truck driver and he was my teacher. As I tell people, I learned at an early age and from the best.

My mother and I are road warriors without fear of car trouble or bad weather. We have been known to pack our bags and head out on a road trip when the forecast for bad weather should have made us stay home. Our travel motto is "hope for the best." We did get caught in a bad snowstorm a few years ago and both of my sons were ready to give us the lecture on age and maturity, etc. I now quote them: "2 women in the Senior Citizen category, heading out on an 8 hour trip, in a car built in 1989 (also a Senior Citizen named Ethel), when there is a snow storm predicted should have their car keys taken away from them"! Mother, Ethel (the car) and I finally got there all in one piece and in hindsight I agree it was a bit fool hardy of us to start out when we did. I would rather refer to it as a bad case of judgment rather than "crazy". But without the snow experience it wouldn't have been an adventure, right? Someday when my mother is no longer able to travel, we will look back on these road trips and remember all of the adventures we had. Those memories will give both us **Southern Comfort.**

"Are we there yet?"

Southern Comfort...
Name That Car

I cannot swear that this is a unique habit to the South but I think that it is. I do know first hand that it happens in my family so I will share this with you. We name our cars. We never just refer to the new car as THE CAR. Depending on the cars personality and /or the driver's attitude the new car will be given a name.

My mother's 1989 Crown Vic is named Ethel because the car is a full figured vehicle and will only use premium (Ethel) grade gasoline. Ethel will not change her habit of only having the best fuel and will cough, sputter and act-up if she is feed anything but the best. My mother, Lois, bought Ethel when Ethel was brand new and they have been hard & fast friends for almost 20 years. Ethel must really love her diet because she has been almost trouble free all of her life and when we see the new car advertisements for cars with guarantees of 25 miles per gallon it makes us laugh. Ethel gets 26-28 mpg on road trips and she's got 130,000 miles on her speedometer. Not bad huh? Do the math and you will see that she is truly one of the cars that you can say "was only driven to Church on Sunday". Of course she also goes to the local drugstore, the beauty shop, a drive thru window at several different fast food restaurants, and occasionally to the bank. She is our vehicle of choice when we take road trips. She is big and roomy with comfortable seats, sub zero air-conditioning, and a wonderful sound system even if she doesn't have a CD player (CD was not even in the English language when she was built unless you were talking about a Certificate of Deposit at the local bank), and you feel like you are riding down the highway in an EZ boy recliner. I think she enjoys going fast on the interstate when we take a trip. I can almost hear her going "whee" when she gets to use all 8 cylinders!

Ethel and Lois do have a few communication issues which have resulted in the 2 of them being pulled over by the police. They were cited for weaving and the policeman asked mother if she had been drinking. My mother assured the young policeman that the strongest beverage she had that day was a glass of iced tea. The weaving was not "really weaving"...it was *floating* because Ethel could not decide which lane was the best. I would love to have a video of this to send to the police academy for Senior Citizen training. The young policeman asked mother to be more careful and to get a firm "grip" on Ethel before she caused an accident. He was not wanting a repeat of the "Ethel and Lois" *floating* routine any time soon! Last year mother and Ethel were involved in 2 accidents. One was their fault and the other was not. The first one involved them *killing* an innocent tire that was mounted on the back of the vehicle in front of them while they were in the drive thru lane at her favorite fast food window. Ethel *forgot* to stop quickly enough and rear-ended the SUV in front of her. Oddly enough the front headlight on Ethel matched up perfectly with the tire mounted on the back of the SUV and when the headlight glass broke from the impact it "speared" the tire. That tire was dead in just a few minutes! Mother called to tell me what had happened and to tell me that *Ethel* was *a tire killer.*

The 2nd accident happened when an elderly gentlemen side-swiped Ethel as he was pulling out into traffic. He asked mother if she was okay and she replied that she was fine but Ethel was hurt. He and his wife kept looking into mother's car to find Ethel. He told mother that he simply did not see her car when he pulled out and she replied that if he could not see a car the size of Ethel that he needed to stop driving! That statement let the light bulb come on and he realized who/what Ethel was and why she was "hurt". Lois and Ethel will continue as the dynamic duo until mother finally gives up her set of car keys and becomes just a passenger instead of a driver. In a very few more years Ethel will be eligible to get the special vintage auto license plate. That will definitely be a proud day for our family.

My granddaddy had a Morris Minor convertible. It's an English brand of car and it had several owners before he adopted it. He called it the Doodle Bug and they were friends for many years. It had a gearshift mounted in the floor and it needed first gear replaced. If you put it in first gear the grinding noise would make you wince. The solution was to "skip" that gear and use 2nd gear and just give it a little extra gas when you started to move. A family friend worked as an upholsterer at a casket company. He offered to make new seat covers and

1 of them would travel all over town running errands
and visiting family. This experience also taught my
young son the power of overcoming physical
obstacles. His great-granddaddy could have been
bitter about his health problem but instead he just
learned to adapt and he never complained. People
would see him and the Doodle Bug coming and
wave. He was too busy driving and shifting to wave
back so he would just give them his friendly nod as
a response. As a side note to this driving
experience...the great-grandson, who learned to

shift gears to help his great-granddaddy, bought a new car years later and for whatever reason he did not actually drive the new car. He picked out the color combination that he liked and told the salesman to do the paperwork. When the salesman delivered the new car to him after all of the money had changed hands, my son discovered that he had just purchased a 5 speed and not the automatic that he thought he was buying. He was so stunned that he did not say a word to the salesman and drove that 5 speed for 2 years before he traded it in on a car that an automatic transmission. Thank goodness he had learned to shift and clutch all of those years before or he would have had to call someone to come and drive him and his new "you have to shift gears car" home! Mia was a very sweet little convertible and she served him well even if she did come with that one little surprise.

My oldest son Michael has a vintage Mercedes convertible. She is named Edna Banks. She is not as flashy as her cousin the newest version of this model. To my son she looked like an Edna when he bought her. Reasonable, smart, good looking in a nice way, dependable...all of the reasons to think of her as an old fashioned Edna. She is given the best of care and is high maintenance. She is treated like the lady that she is and will probably be a member of our family well into her golden years. The last name of Banks is because she cost so much!

I have a 4-door pick-up truck that is named Mr. T because it is full sized and isn't afraid of anything. His little sister, our other vehicle, is a small car that we named Sylvie. She is very sweet tempered and has never given us one bit of trouble. Unlike her big brother she will run on "cheap" gas and gets great gas mileage.

My parents bought full size station wagons to travel in with 3 children and one time my dad bought us a Lincoln town car complete with all of the new gadgets for the 1962 model. That was back when the Lincoln was a huge vehicle! The Lincoln was wider and longer than the station wagon we had. It was so long and big that when it was parked in our carport the fins on the back-end were not even under the roof of the carport. That car was called "big Link" and it truly lived up to its name. I guess it was the Lincoln version of the Hummer before we thought of a Hummer as anything except a vehicle for the armed forces. I know we always felt like we were riding around in a very pretty tank!

My youngest son has had several pick-up trucks and his favorite color is red. His first vehicle was "old red" which was a very used truck that we bought 2nd hand, "new red" eventually replaced "old red" and the last red truck was "big red" because it was a bigger vehicle than the other red trucks had been. He is not sentimental on picking names but just picked a name that suited the vehicle. We should have named "old red", his very used pick up truck, the "Skeeter Killer". Old Red had a very bad oil ring leak and when Stephen started it the smoke would just boil out of the tail pipe killing every mosquito within a mile! Very useful in the SE Arkansas Delta where we lived but just a wee bit embarrassing to a teenager. That old truck ran good once it "cleared its throat" and that was the most important thing to my son and killing a few skeeters wasn't bad either!

As you can see all of us have an affectionate side for our vehicles. We find a car or truck that suits us and we stay with it. We enjoy the familiar and reliable and it gives us **Southern Comfort** to turn the key in the ignition and head on down the highway.

"Fill her up please. Ethel only uses premium gas. She has her standards to uphold. Nothing cheap about Ethel!"

Southern Comfort...
Garden Hose

On hot, humid summer days there is nothing better than an afternoon of water fun. With so many homes having swimming pools today I wonder if the art of running thru the sprinkler is now a thing of the past? I can remember when I was a youngster, and yes we did have running water inside and outside the house, the only "real" swimming pools we had in our town were the public pool, the pool at the country club and the pool at the VFW. Some of us had the 3 ring blow up pools and a very few people had 3 feet deep above ground pools. The above ground pools had a metal outer shell and a vinyl liner. When the summer was over and it was time to take down the pool for the winter the grass under the pool had a very unpleasant odor. I hated that part of summer when everything was officially over and the pool was put up for another year.

Cleaning the vinyl liner was not any fun either, even if your mom did supply you with plenty of soap and the garden hose and tell you " *have fun*".

Very few, if any, homes in our small town had in-ground swimming pools. Today in some neighborhoods every back yard will have a "real" pool and most of the pools have water slides. My granddaughter has access to 2 of these real pools and one is right next-door at her aunt's house. She is going to grow up thinking going swimming in a real pool is *"no big deal"*. It will never be as special to her as it was to me because of the easy access that she has.

I am going to spend some *fun time* with my granddaughter in a couple of weeks and I intend to teach her about the fun side of the garden hose. When we get finished the carport and everything else we can find to wash down outside will be *"all clean"*. We can also wash the outside toys, her wagon, and even the big dog if we can get him to cooperate. Swimming is one thing but playing with the garden hose is a completely different water sport. Running barefoot thru wet grass and dancing in and out of the sprinkler will be a fun way to spend the afternoon. All of that water makes a child thirsty so it will require at least one Popsicle while we are outside. No worry about the Popsicle dripping on anything, you are already wet.

My children grew up playing on the Slip & Slide and with the Water Willy. When neither of these was available just a plain garden hose would be just fine. One of the things we liked to do was to put our finger over the end of the garden hose and see how far we could spray the water. Using a real nozzle was cheating!

The circulating round sprayer is fun to jump in and out of and all of that water swirling up into the sky and the sun dancing thru it making little rainbows is a wonderful thing to see. The worst thing that can happen during an afternoon of garden hose fun is that you get wet. No fear of drowning or getting too hot or falling and hurting something. Playing with the garden hose is just good clean fun. All you need for clean up is a dry towel and sunshine.

Anytime you need a dose of cheap Southern summer fun go turn on the garden hose and let your children entertain themselves and you with a few hours of squirting water and playing in the sun. I guarantee it will put a smile on your face watching your child squealing and splashing. If that does not give your heart **Southern Comfort** with a little twist of "*wet*" you need to start packing and move to a colder climate!

"*Weather for today...hot and humid! Enjoy the sunshine!!*"

Southern Comfort... Simple Ingredients

In the South we have specialty dishes that are truly unique to our area of the world. My daughter-in-law has introduced me to chocolate gravy and buttermilk biscuits. Most small towns do not have a donut shop and even if they do and you live 20 miles out of town running into town most mornings is not an option. Thus the chocolate gravy and biscuit meal to satisfy that sweet tooth and give you something that will stick to the ribs longer than a donut. It also is very effective in preventing wrinkles as I stated earlier in the book. If you live on a farm in the South you learn to substitute and to make things that require very few ingredients. Chocolate in all of its forms is always a staple in the Southern pantry. As long as your pantry has chocolate, flour and pecans you are ready to bake something that will cover your craving for something sweet.

All Southern cooks have their own special Karo pecan (pronounced pah kahn—not pee can) pie recipe. Add a spoonful of whiskey to give it a little kick or chocolate chips to turn it into Derby Pie and with very little effort you now have 3 different versions of your basic recipe. The most important ingredient of course is the Pecan portion of the ingredients. Bad, dried out, bitter pecans are just plain nasty!

My mother-in-law could make the best pies and she would bake up several pie-crusts at the same time for "just in case" moments. They could become chocolate pie or coconut pie in a very few minutes. She usually had some pecans in the freezer that she could roast in the oven as something a little special when people came for dinner.

My grandparents lived in the same house for almost 50 years and had big pecan trees in the back yard. There are several varieties of pecans and they grew paper shell long skinny pecans. Every fall my granddaddy would put on his big pocket apron and gather his pecan crop. He did not like using the fancy pecan picker that one of us gave him. He preferred the bend-over-and-pick-them-up-by-hand method. One year my 5-year old son was his assistant and he learned the value of pecans that year. At the end of the day the 2 of them would take the freshly gathered pecans to the NUT HOUSE to swap them for cracked pecans. We had a pecan cracker but it was a lot easier to go to the NUT HOUSE and just swap out and bring home pecans that were ready to shell. We would spend hours each evening watching television and shelling pecans. Of course, part of the "crop" had to pass the taste test during the shelling process. I have bought very expensive grocery store pecans and they never have that some wonderful taste as the ones that we had back then. The end result of all of that labor was definitely worth it because the memory of the taste of fresh pecans has stayed with me all of these years.

In some parts of the South the peanut is King. Not in my part of the South...the pecan reigns supreme. Pecan brittle, millionaire candy (a combination of Kraft caramels, Pet milk and Hershey chocolate) banana pudding with chopped pecans sprinkled on top, pie crust made with crushed pecans added to the flour, pancakes, waffles and of course Banana Nut Bread made with pecans, not walnuts. All of these are favorites at my house. If you have a few soda crackers, egg white, sugar and chopped pecans you can also make a cracker pie. See what I mean about just needing a few basic ingredients? Add chopped pecans to chicken salad and you have just elevated that dish from chicken with mayo and relish to divine chicken salad. If you do not have pecans stored in the freezer or the pantry your cupboards are bare!

One of the easiest vegetables to grow is the tomato. You need a few feet of good soil that gets plenty of sunshine and has good drainage. A large barrel filled with dirt can be substituted if you only have a patio or deck if you don't have room in the yard. All you need to grow tomatoes is good dirt, water, plenty of sunshine, a little Miracle Grow, the cage to hold the plant up when it starts to get heavy from the fruit, and healthy starter plants. I have friends and family who swear that nothing tastes as good as a home-grown tomato. They make the best BLT sandwich and the small ones make great homemade Rotel.

The other day I heard a sales clerk in our local grocery store tell a customer that she did not know what Rotel was! I politely asked the young clerk where she was from and was not surprised to hear her say that she was from California.

Rotel and Velveeta Cheese are as important to a Southern pantry as milk and bread. Children grow up learning to eat cheese dip and chips while watching their Saturday morning cartoons. The best Rotel is the homemade variety that is made with fresh ingredients. All you need are a few tomatoes, some jalapeno peppers, some onion, salt, pepper and a drop of hot sauce. You can add as many of the jalapeno peppers as you want depending on the "burn factor" you want to achieve. Combine this with a stick of butter, a box of Velveeta Cheese and heat until everything is melted and bubbling. Grab a big bag of Fritos or Doritos, a large cold beverage and enjoy!

One year we had an ice storm that caused a town wide power outage. For several days the entire town was without electricity so we learned to adapt. I had an all-electric home so that meant cooking on the out-door grill was my only option. I got my big heavy cast iron pot and filled it with all of the ingredients to make cheese dip. I stood in the cold, bundled up from head to toe, and stirred that pot. It was worth every shiver. Hot cheese dip with chips on a stormy, bitterly cold winter day took some of the gloom away and definitely provided **Southern Comfor**t when we really needed it!

"Can I have just one more piece of pah-kahn pie please?"

Southern Comfort...
Come on In

In the South you'll hear the greeting *"come on in"* when you knock on a friends door. The wonderful thing about a Southerner saying, *"come on in"* is that they mean that and the rest of the phrase is *"and make yourself at home"*. If you show up at mealtime you will immediately be included and told to "pull up a chair". There is always room for one more at Southern dinner tables. Having one more mouth to feed may involve the hostess making another batch of biscuits so that everyone will have enough but that is just taken for granted on her part and nothing unusual. I had an uncle who loved leftover cold biscuits and our house had a metal biscuit keeper and it always sat on the counter top in the kitchen and he knew it. We could always count on him to "snag" a biscuit or 2 when he was there for a visit.

Southern health note on the value of buttermilk biscuits: they will settle an upset stomach if you wash them down with a Coca Cola. I use them instead of antacids at my house and they sure do test better than chewing up a chalky tablet!

My uncle knew he was always welcome to eat anything we had and he returned the love when we went to his house. The minute you walked in the door he would ask you if you were hungry or needed something to drink. He did more than just ask. He always headed for the kitchen and quizzed my aunt on what was in the refrigerator to feed these hungry people.

A Southern hostess always has a few quick recipes up her sleeve. Cracker Pie, homemade Southern Banana Pudding, Hot Fudge Cake and Sloppy Joes can always be put together in a hurry and with very few ingredients. If nothing else is available ice cream floats with whatever beverage is in the house usually will finish off a good meal with something sweet.

One of my favorite memories from my youth is my grandmother's driveway that was lined with beautiful Mimosa trees. The message that driveway said to me was "come on in" and "your grandmother is going to be glad to see you". The flowering trees provided the driveway with shade and beauty and welcomed you. My grandmother had a green thumb on both hands and she had rose bushes and what I always called snowball bushes in the front of the house next to the front porch. We love flowering shrubs and the fragrant gardenia bush is a favorite with all good Southern families. My granddaddy had a gardenia bush blooming under his bedroom window so that he could smell it every night before he went to bed and smell it again the first thing when he woke up the next morning. Not having air conditioning helped you appreciate the wonderful smells of the roses, lilac bushes and the gardenias.

A bubbling fountain at the front entrance is another welcome for visitors and family. I have several friends who decorate the walkway and front door with lavish wreathes and floral arrangements. They invite you into their home with beauty that starts before you open the front door. We want the outside of our homes to make family and visitors feel that they are welcome and that this home is one where you can always find love and comfort. We are not inclined to have cookie cutter housing with all of the homes looking the same.

In the South we name our homes even if it is just known in the community as the Smith House. In our glorious past we had homes with proud names like Tara and 12 Oaks from Gone with the Wind and today some of these beautiful old homes are still standing and standing proud. We have several homes in the Charleston area that are now true Southern treasures and are open as museums or are maintained with pride as family homes. No matter the size of the home just knowing that it is there just waiting for you when you are tired and weary brings us comfort.

Going home to momma's house always gives us a sense of **Southern Comfort** even if we are old enough to retire and start drawing our social security checks. I can remember the sound my footsteps made when I crossed my grandmothers wooden front porch. That sound let me know that I was back home and going into a house that would always be a place of love and refuge.

Welcome Home, Home Coming, Honey I'm Home, Home cooked meal, Home for the holidays...just say the words and they bring instant comfort. We bring the baby home from the hospital and by the time they are able to converse with their mom and dad they know what the word "*home*" means. We instill that love of home and the knowledge that this is where you will find love and comfort and shelter at the very beginning of their lives. They know that they can always come home and find someone there who loves them.

It is not just the creature comforts that we seek. We know that home is our "nest", our safe place when the rest of the world is going crazy. I admit that I enjoy coming back home to my own bed. I can sleep in a 5 star hotel and I still yearn for my own bed and am relieved when I finally get back home to my bedroom. When I travel I take my own pillow and my son-in-law takes his bedside fan and his pillow. My oldest son takes his silk comforter that has definitely seen better days, if he can fit it into his suitcase. It is amazing what we decide we cannot live without even for a few short days.

We all seek comfort in things that are familiar. My sister when she was an infant would not sleep any place except in her own bed. You could take the bed with you and that would work but she had to have that bed, end of discussion. I could sleep any place and evidently did from the stories they tell me. My granddaughter is a "sleep anywhere" child and as long as she wakes up the next morning to a familiar face she is happy with the accommodations. She adapts very well and knows that she is safe if she has a loved one with her.

I grew up hearing Judy Garland singing "Over the Rainbow" and watched The Wizard of Oz more than once. When she clicks the heels of the ruby red slippers and chants "there is no place like home" she is wishing what all of us want to wish when we are away from home...we just want to go home. No matter what you do, where you live or even how you live, home is always precious. In the South we enjoy having company and our welcome mat is always out. A favorite expression is ***"Make yourself at Home"*** and we really mean it. Home is **Southern Comfort** at the highest level.

"Honey, I'm home!"

Southern Comfort...
Let There Be Light

In the South traditions start and we do not even realize it at the time. When I bought my first home it had a beautiful cut crystal chandelier in the dining room. Once I saw it hanging in that room I knew I had to have it. It was truly love at first sight. I negotiated the price of the home to allow them to leave the chandelier. Since that purchase many years ago this chandelier has had many road trips. We fondly refer to it as "the traveling light show".

I had professional movers crate it when I moved out of the first home and it remained in the crate, lonely and unlit for 2 years. I finally moved into a home that would accommodate a chandelier and it was my dining room chandelier for a few years until I moved again. Back to the crate it went and would have remained there but it was now time to start many road trips with my oldest son Michael. He never seems to live in the same house for more than a couple of years. Thanks to his many moves that beautiful chandelier has traveled from Arkansas to Kentucky; back to Arkansas, then to Texas followed by Alabama and presently it is shedding light in my son's home in Florida. It has already moved to 3 different homes in Florida but at least it stayed in the same town. My son has taken it down, packed it and then put it back up so many times that it is as easy as 1,2,3. It continues to provide beautiful light and when my son goes house hunting his list of "must haves" includes a dining room for the chandelier. When I bought it all of those years ago it was expensive and with all of the years of travel and memories it has gone from expensive to priceless. It will always represent home and give my son **Southern Comfort.**

"I'll leave the light on for you!"

Southern Comfort...
Shall We Dance?

Ladies in dresses with big hoop skirts, men in dress suits and highly polished boots, music playing...just close your eyes and picture it. It was a time of good manners, white gloves, the curtsey, the bow, and a peck on the cheek or a kiss on the back of the hand. It was a time of formal dancing which required both partners to "know the steps". The young ladies had a dance card and the young gentlemen politely asked if they could have their name listed next to a dance.

This was years before we had electricity, Boise sound systems, rap and Elvis and the only twist anyone knew about was not something associated with music.

The ballrooms were filled with candlelight, live music, wooden floors, sweet cold punch for the beverage, and chaperons to watch over these young people to keep everything "proper". Those were the dances of the South years and years ago.

Today we still have *coming out* balls for young Southern ladies where they are all thought of as a Southern Princess for that evening. This new generation of young men and women of the South know the dance ritual and for a brief moment of time bring a part of the old South alive again. You can almost see the ghosts of the dancers from the past watching over them.

The *coming out* ball is their official debut into the time in their life when they are actively looking for the husband who will be their partner for the rest of the life. Once these young women of the South start the *courting ritual* their mothers smile and watch and are so proud. Mother and daughter are now dreaming of the beautiful parties and the wedding that will be in the future. The daddies start standing guard duty over their little darlins and worry every time she walks out the door with a new beau on her arm. Their little girl is not little anymore and now the sleepless nights begin until she is safely returned to her own room each night.

This love of dance and having a dance partner for life is something to really watch and enjoy. I enjoy going to a dance where there are several generations on the dance floor. I visited a casino in Tunica, MS last year and a dance couple was stealing the show on the dance floor. No, they were not break dancing. They were doing the swing and they really knew how to do it. I would guess their age to be late 70's but they still had the moves. They must have been partners for many years because she seemed to anticipate where he would want them to go next. It was a joy to watch them being "young again".

There is a hotel in Memphis that has a long and wonderful history. It is called the Peabody Hotel in downtown Memphis and is famous for the live ducks that parade in and out of the lobby everyday to swim in the big fountain. The hotel has been refurbished many times and is still as grand as it ever was. You can feel the years of warmth and comfort that this hotel has given to everyone who has been lucky enough to check-in for the night. Nothing frantic, nothing high speed, everything is laid back, slow and comforting.

On the roof there is a ballroom that has been enjoyed since the hotel first opened. My mother spent many wonderful times at this ballroom and it was not just a ballroom with great music. It had a glass roof that could be opened and you could dance under the stars. Talk about romantic! I think that puts it at the top of my list.

Visiting such a wonderful place, seeing the horse drawn carriages on the brick lined streets, listening to the music from Beale Street, smelling the BBQ being enjoyed at the Rendezvous in the alley across the street, all of this makes a Southern girl or guy smile. This is truly **Southern Comfort.**

Come on in! The food is hot, the drinks are cold and the band is playing "your song"!!

Southern Comfort...
Shelling Peas

In the South, during the late summer days, there is a sound that is as soothing as it is productive. It is the sound of plink, plink, plink that peas and beans make as they are being shelled and the fruit goes into a flat bottom pan or bowl. Southerners love peas...black eye, whippoorwill, purple hull, Crowder...we love them all.

A big "mess of" fresh peas cooked with a little ham or bacon for seasoning, a big iron skillet of buttermilk cornbread, a fresh-from-the-garden sliced tomato, some freshly pulled green onions and of course, a big glass of iced sweet tea and you have a meal to remember. This is a meal anyone in the South would be proud to serve to family and/ or company. We do not think of it as a "meatless" meal because of the ham or bacon used in the peas for flavoring.

The shelling process brings the family together since it is not gender or age specific. Little kids grow up learning the fine art of shelling peas. Boys, as well as girls, are included in this training process. The trick to successful pea shelling is to get everything lined up just right. This means getting all of your "equipment" correctly positioned. Depending on which side is your dominant side this is the way you line everything up: Grocery bag of peas to shell sitting on the floor on your dominant side, flat bottom metal pan or bowl in your lap, bucket or garbage can on your other side. Now the shelling can begin. You need to find yourself a comfortable place to sit since sitting is required. You can choose a comfy couch, a rocker, a swing on the front porch; lawn chairs in the back yard...just get comfortable. If you want to have true family time go someplace other than in front of the television. This is an opportunity to talk with your spouse, your children, your grandchildren, your mother. As I said before it is an equal opportunity chore and everyone can join in without worrying that they "won't do it right". As far as I know there really is no wrong or right or a quota that says you are a good worker. Just make sure that you do not leave any of the peas in the shell and avoid crushing any in the process and that is all that is expected. Once you get your rhythm going you can do a big bag in about 30 minutes and not loose one minute of conversation time. Just so you will know...purple hull peas are called purple for a very good reason. The hull is purple and if you are hands are the least bit wet they will get stained from handling the hulls.

When there is a bumper crop the whole family pitches in and gets the peas ready to go into freezer bags and get stored in the freezer until they are ready to cook. Shelling is never a race to see who can finish first. It is meant to be slow and steady with a good flow of conversation included in the process. You get immediate results and the gentle plink of the peas hitting your container will let you know that you are doing a good job. Clean up is easy and only requires a big trash bag. The peas just get poured directly into the freezer bags and put into the freezer. Oh so simple and oh so good!

In the dead of winter, when summer is just a memory, nothing will give you **Southern Comfort** like sitting down to a dinner that includes peas from the garden. Even if the temperature outside is 10 below freezing those peas will taste just as good as they did when it was 100 degrees in the shade.

"So, what did you do today? How was school? Do you think the football team will win this Friday? What do you want me to fix for supper tomorrow night to go with the peas? Thank you for sitting, shelling and talking to me. It's nice to catch up."

Southern Comfort...
Singing in the Choir

Most of you already know that the South is in what is referred to as the Bible Belt. Southern Baptist out numbers all of the other denominations in our bigger cities. But even in our small towns we usually have a good representation of all religions. In the smaller towns we combine our youth groups for special events so that everyone who can attend is included. I always think that makes these events even more special since no one is turned away.

For a couple of years I lived in a very, very small town in Arkansas. The town didn't even have a flashing yellow light much less a real stoplight. The town was small but in addition to the Baptist Church and Methodist Church this little town had a Presbyterian Church. It was built in the 1940's and had never been remodeled. It had been "freshened up" from time to time with new paint as needed but other than that it was the original in every way. You entered the front double doors into the small foyer and then went directly into the sanctuary. You entered at the front of the sanctuary instead of the rear. I guess this was designed in the hope that the congregation would seat themselves closer to the pastor instead of in the back rows. It apparently was a good plan because the front rows would fill up and only the back half of the church was empty. The pulpit and the choir loft were in the front of the church so the pastor greeted everyone as they entered instead of just when they left. The church has some of the most beautiful stained glass windows that provide droplets of color shining in the room when the sun shines thru them.

The seating capacity could not be more than 70 or 80 people and we very rarely even had half that many to attend Sunday morning service. The church had been without a musician for such a long time that when they found out that I could play the piano I felt obligated to do my best. It had been years since I played the piano and it had been even longer than that since I last played a pipe organ. I hoped that with Gods' help I could play good enough to make all of us make a joyful sound. It took me a few months to get over the stage fright of just playing before that many people but finally I decided to see if the big organ and I could be friends. It truly is a magnificent instrument with pipes that must reach heaven. The first Sunday the congregation realized that I was at the organ instead of the piano was a surprise to all of us. It was a struggle but after a few months I grew to love it. The organist sits with her back to the congregation and I had a little rear view mirror attached to the side of the organ so I could see what was happening behind my back.

One Sunday that little mirror came in very handy. I had a toddler son who was my helper when we went to church to practice. He would sit up on the bench with me until he got tired of *making music* and then he would get down and go play with his toys. He eventually knew every nook and cranny of that church. One Sunday he *escaped* from the nursery, walked from the back of the church all the way past the preacher (who did his best to catch him), climbed the stairs up to the choir loft and then seated himself next to me at the organ. The congregation had stopped singing before he got there but I already knew he was headed my way by sneaking a peak into the mirror. **Southern Comfort** to him was to sit next to his momma and nobody was going to stop him before he got to me.

That year we had several exchange students living with different families in our congregation. Because of this the church actually had a youth group for the first time in years. I decided to put this bunch of talented young people and a few adults to work and we became a Sunday choir on Easter Sunday. We borrowed choir robes from one of the bigger churches, borrowed music from them as well, and we practiced and practiced. Two of the students were musicians and so was my oldest son so I had solo opportunities for all three of them. We had a trumpet and French horn duet to start one of the anthems we sang and I don't think Gabriel could have done better himself. When the choir marched in and filled up the choir loft for the first time in many, many years my husband heard two of the "little old ladies" in the congregation remark that the choir must be rented. To their surprise my husband informed them that everyone up there was from that church. That was the only Sunday that I ever got to turn the volume UP on that beautiful organ. I can remember hearing it swell with pride! We had a full house, with every pew filled with family and friends who came for the special day. That Sunday morning we filled the air with beautiful music and I was so proud of my volunteer choir. Just remembering the joy in their voices and the smiles on the faces of the congregation gives my heart **Southern Comfort** that I know that I will never forget.

You don't have to be the biggest choir in town...you just have to give it your all and do your best and the good Lord will take care of the rest.

And the angels joined in the chorus!

Southern Comfort...
Dancers in the Sky...
Up, up and Away

When you see these air planes take off and land so effortlessly, climb straight up into the sky, zoom close to the ground, do the *"limbo"* under power lines, do *"dips"* as they come up and down, *"shimmy"* up the side of tall trees, it is a wonderful dance to watch and appreciate. The **"dancing air planes"** that I just described are the modern day version of the crop dusters now called Ag Planes. The pilots of old had to have nerves of steel, good piloting skills and a love of flying. The modern day Ag pilot has to have all of those skills and more. Today's Ag planes fly so fast and carry so much cargo that the Ag Pilot has to be physically and mentally fit at all times. The dollars involved in the price of the plane plus all of the money the farmer has invested in the cargo makes this a very high dollar, high risk occupation. Every load is valuable cargo and costs thousands of dollars.

On an early morning in mid-April you can hear the birds calling to each other.

The butterflies are flying from flower to flower and the temperature is in the warm but not hot zone. Now is the time you hear the roar of the engine as the Ag Pilot starts his day. Conditions are perfect for flying. The sun is shining and the wind has taken a rest so everything is calm and still.

A good Ag Pilot can make numerous trips during the morning. Taking off and landing his plane is 2nd nature to him...just like walking and breathing. The ground crew loads the cargo, the plane takes off, the pilot does his dance in the sky, returns to the air strip, lands the plane and refills his cargo and is ready for another trip in the sky. He will continue this process until the natural heating process from the spring sun creates enough wind to cause him to shut down for a few hours. Around late evening when the earth is starting to cool down he can resume his work for the day. An Ag Pilot works as many hours as are necessary in that day. He does not get paid overtime for working more than 8 hours a day and his work rule for each day is definitely to keep working until it is too dark to do more or until he is finally finished with all of the applications that he needs to do for that day. Mother Nature is not a lady you can trust to give you the same great weather conditions tomorrow that you had today.

The modern, advanced Ag plane and all of its equipment has evolved almost as much as the model T has to today's luxury automobiles. Today's AG pilot has a plane so much faster than the crop duster had 25 years ago which is both good and bad. Today's Ag plane can carry much bigger and heavier loads and the plane itself is heavier even without a load of chemicals on board. The speed had to increase to allow for the heavier loading capacity. To soar thru the air at such high speed and duck under power lines and around trees takes great skill mentally and physically. The new planes have so many extras that the pilot has to be up-to-date on the latest technology to stay in business. Up until a few years ago the farmer had to send a flag person to the field when the chemicals or seed were being flown on but with the new GPS system that is no longer necessary. I can remember seeing grown men jump down between rows because the pilot was too close and they were being sprayed with seed or chemical. With the new technology the load can be dispersed more accurately which increases the results of the fertilizer or chemicals being applied. A good Ag Pilot is worth every dollar he charges to a farmer. His services are critical to the success of the farmer's crop.

Most Ag Pilots are 2nd or 3rd generation and have known the business all of their lives. It is not an occupation that you would "just decide to do". Neither is farming...both are occupations that are family based. Farmers know who the really good Ag Pilots are and become hard and fast friends as well as business associates. A mistake by the pilot is always costly both financially and emotionally. A really good Ag Pilot can count his mistakes on one hand and hopefully on only one finger of that hand.

When you are in the big airports, the pilots and staff for national airlines all have on their fancy uniforms. The Ag Pilot does not need or want a fancy uniform. He is not going to be sitting in an air-conditioned cockpit with plenty of leg-room. He is going to be strapped into his seat and most of the cockpits are built to be tight.

If the Ag Pilot is lucky the temperature in his cockpit will only go as high as 95 degrees but more than likely on a hot summer day that 95 will quickly climb to 105. That is when the physically fit part of the job description is put to the test.

The pilot's ability to read his gauges, judge distance and conditions is as impressive as anything that a major airline pilot faces. This is when the part of the job description about being mentally fit becomes vitally important.

The Ag Pilot does not have many safety features to protect him if he makes a mistake. His agility and level of concentration is awesome. He knows his plane and is truly one with it. You have seen the cartoon with Snoopy and the Red Baron. None of these Ag Pilots are Snoopy. All of them are equal to the Red Baron! Accidents do happen every year and sometimes when you see what is left of the plane you realize that the pilot's guardian angel was truly riding in the cockpit with the pilot.

These dare devil pilots are beautiful to watch as they soar thru the air, swoop down low, dive straight up to avoid a tree, dive under power lines and do all of the many maneuvers required of them each day. They look like big birds doing what they love to do best...soaring thru the sky!

The rest of the USA has astronauts. The South has our own "men of the air". They are called Ag Pilots. In the rural South we grow up watching these daring young men take off into the sky in their powerful planes day after day and it becomes a natural thing for us to see. When you leave that area and return for a visit you realize what you were taking for granted is very special and wonderful to watch.

Southern Comfort comes at the end of a busy day when the pilot and plane are both safely back on the ground and the log-book shows hundreds of acres that are now treated with beneficial chemicals or fertilizer. The sun is beginning to set and now it is time for the pilot to go home to a hot meal and show some **Southern Comfort** loving to his family.

"Jason can make that plane go anywhere! He makes it look so easy. Fast, powerful, quick, and wonderful to watch."

Southern Comfort...
Playing Games

In the South playing card games is 2nd nature to us. Southern children learn to play Go Fish and eventually work their way up to Rook, Canasta, Bridge or Pinochle. The game of Rook is challenging without taking such a high degree of concentration that it interferes with the social part of the evening. Playing Bridge and sometimes Canasta can be so intense, the degree of concentration so high, that you can not even enjoy a cold drink or some chips and dip. You certainly cannot carry on a gossip-based conversation without it resulting in you and your partner having a very low score.

Cheating within a family game is expected. It is usually done right out in the open, like the way my grandmother cheated when she was partnered with my granddaddy. She felt obligated to "help" him pick the color for trumps. There are 4 colors in Rook and if she said, "Owen, it sure is dark outside tonight" that was her "help" to him to call Black as the trump color. We would scold her and she would just shrug and laugh.

My parents were so addicted to their weekly Bridge game and friends that we would travel back to West Memphis from Louisville at least once a month. It took them a couple of years to reconnect with another card group in Louisville so we spent many hours on the road going back and forth from our new home city to our old home city. My daddy would even play at the ladies table when they were one person short and he was home for the day. He did request that they not serve him "lady food"! If tuna and a tomato were lunch he expected his tuna and tomato to be put on a sandwich and not served as a salad.

Playing cards with the adults taught me to count my numbers, remember the cards that had been played, to win or loose with grace, and to keep my mouth shut. Doing that last part was never easy for me, but I wanted to play badly enough, that I learned to *"be quiet and be still"* at a very early age.

My parents also loved to play a dice game called Wahoo. The game was a home-made version that involved making the playing board out of wood. My dad was never a carpenter, I am not sure he even knew which end of a hammer to use, so one of the other men graciously made us our board. It takes 4 people to play at each table and you are partnered with the person seated across from you. You play as a 2-person team and you have to roll a certain number to enter the board to start your marble around the board. Just choosing the correct dice and the color of your marbles could cause major discussion among the players. Some colors were considered lucky and some of the dice were considered "*hot*". Once all of that was finally settled the game could begin. Several times my parents had 3 tables playing at our house with all of my aunts and uncles as the team members. It could get pretty *cut throat* to be just a simple game and it can really get competitive. My 2 grown sons have had to be separated because their *enthusiasm* got a little out of hand. They understood the "*cut throat*" version immediately!

Years later I made Wahoo boards to give as gifts to friends and one Saturday night I was the hostess for a Sr. High Sunday School party. It was "Bring an Adult to Play Night" and the game was Wahoo. Each of the teenagers had to bring either a parent or another adult of their choice. That night I had 8 teenagers and 8 adults paired up into teams and it was a night I will never forget. Once they figured out how to play aggressively the fun really began. My neighbor across the street asked mc the next morning what we had been doing to have people yelling out numbers so loudly that she could hear them across the street? I told her it was all clean and innocent fun...not gambling...just Wahoo. The next morning at church I was happy to see the adults and the teenagers acknowledge each other with a smile.

To connect one generation to another is not complicated. All it takes is some food, cold drinks, and the Wahoo boards. It is a simple game that allows for a lot of conversation and no fancy rules that you have to remember.

As a side note on the benefits of this exchange...A prominent business leader was involved with this same group of teenagers when I sponsored a Halloween Scavenger Hunt that same year. He and his wife were leaders of one of the teams of teens. My son was assigned to that team and he saw a relaxed, competitive, fun side to these adults that he would never have seen without that evening of adventure. Now that my son is grown, guess whom he asks for advice regarding his business? You guessed it. The man who came to my house dressed as a Cone Head, who knows how hard my son has worked and how dependable and honest he is from the time he was a teenager, is the man who now is his friend and advisor. That is **Southern Comfort** at it's best!

"I wasn't cheating. I was just thinking out loud how good it would be if my partner called black for trumps since I have so many black cards in my hand...that's all...just thinking out loud."

Southern Comfort...
Gifts from the Heart

In the South we love, make that LOVE, to surprise our loved ones and friends with gifts from the Heart. It can be as simple as a notepad that we found that has special sayings on each page or it can be expensive and elaborate and come from the jewelry store. To find that gift that will bring a smile and hopefully a hug and a kiss as your reward, is **Southern Comfort** at its' best.

Of course, the hardest people to buy for are the people who already have everything they want or need. That is when you really have to put your thinking cap on and get creative!

I had a wonderful husband who due to complications from diabetes was legally blind at the age of 56. He handled his disability with humor and used his white cane to quote "part the waters" when he was in a crowd. Our first Christmas together I decided to give him back something that the diabetes had taken away so I started my search for a "set of wheels". I found a used golf cart that had been converted into a small pick up truck that was absolutely perfect for my husband. It had 4 wheels, a roof, a key for the ignition, and a cargo bed in the back to haul whatever he wanted to put back there so it was exactly the right "vehicle" for him. My youngest son was my pick up and deliveryman and he brought the cart from South East Arkansas to our home the day before Christmas. Santa and her helpers hid the cart across the street in a neighbor's garage until Christmas morning. The next morning after everyone had opened the wrapped gifts there was still one more gift to give...

...*His new wheels*. All of us got dressed to go outside and I told my husband that he had just one more gift and that gift was outside. He was so excited when he saw his gift and he kept saying: "babe, you got me wheels"! When he drove off he didn't allow anyone else to go with him. He just climbed in the drivers seat, turned the key, pushed down on the accelerator and took off!! I started running after him and one of my sons ran the other way to try and catch him on the other side of the circle. When we almost caught him he just waved and kept on going. We lived on a street that curves around a lake and the street has a nice long slope before you get to the lake area. He headed in that direction and we could hear the little wheels screaming as he raced around the lake! That is a morning I will never forget and he enjoyed his little wheels until he died 4 years later. He was born in NYC but that morning he was as Southern as the rest of us, and the joy on his face when he could "drive" again gave all of us a big gift of **Southern Comfort**.

I remember a Christmas when my parents/ Santa Claus gave me a stereo. To be completely honest the word *stereo* should not even apply to what I got that Christmas morning 40 plus years ago. It was a turntable with 2 speakers that could be moved to produce sound on 2 sides of the room as long as the room was very small. You were limited to the length of the wire attached from the speaker to the main body of the record player. The only way it was ever "surround sound" was when we put the speakers in the bathroom and let the tiles on the wall make the sound bigger. Yes, we were definitely ahead of our time and very creative. We woke up that Christmas morning to the sound of Gene Autry singing Rudolph the Red Nosed Reindeer in our hallway. My parents had *stretched* the speakers as far apart as they could to give us the full *stereo* effect. Very, very impressive to children 12 and under!

I played records (yes, I said RECORDS/ 45's and whatever the big ones were numbered) on that stereo for hours each night and listened to Elvis, the Beach Boys, the 4 Seasons, and of course the Supremes. This was years and years before headphones so whatever I was listening to at the time was what everyone in our house got to hear, too. I still have most of those records and when I try and listen to them today I cringe at the quality. Even the records that are in mint condition still sound flat and scratchy. My daddy would listen to one of Eddie Arnold's albums over and over and I still remember most of those songs from that album. This was light years ahead of music channels on cable so what you had in your personal record collection was what you listened to until you saved up enough allowance money to buy a new record. Saving for that next special record made "new music" even more special.

Watching his kids open their presents always was something that my daddy enjoyed. He grew up with so few extras that seeing his family have the things that he never had made him feel proud and happy. Each of us were allowed to open one gift on Christmas Eve so my sister and I worked it out and I would open a box of a certain size and then my sister Becki would open another size box so we actually opened 2 gifts. My daddy would help my little brother to pick out his gift to open so that the 2 of them could play with it before bedtime. One year my brother received a car racing set. Actually I should say my daddy received a car racing set that he was nice enough to let my littler brother play with from time to time. Daddy grew up in a large family and store bought toys were few and far between so when he was able to buy toys for my brother it was like he was making up for some of those "never bought" toys of his youth. Daddy was always a big kid at heart. I can still remember watching him play with my brother and the pure joy on his face and his laughter remain in my heart and memory to this day. It was a moment of **Southern Comfort** that I will always remember!

The year I was 15 my daddy had been sick in the hospital and money was very, very tight at our house. My mother was doing the best that she could to get us Christmas presents but with so many other bills to pay that year there would be very few gifts if any. The Aunts banded together and made sure that we had more than enough pretty things that Christmas. They were my daddy's sisters, and without even knowing it at the time, they provided my daddy with his last Christmas gifts for his children. He died the following year so that Christmas was even more special than any of us realized. It brought my mother and daddy **Southern Comfort** to see us being normal that Christmas after having so many heartache days in the months ahead of Christmas. My daddy's sisters were Southern big-hearted women and they didn't even think twice about filling up the Christmas tree with thoughtful gifts for all of us.

A family tradition that we started a few years ago is Dirty Santa. We play it at Thanksgiving to give the holiday season a *quick start*. Have you ever played Dirty Santa? It can be very funny, wicked and challenging to provide the correct and unique Dirty Santa gift. We have been known to find some of the tackiest gifts that you can buy. One of those was a pole dancing kit complete with costume and CD. The lucky recipient of that truly tacky & unique gift was an elderly lady who actually saw the humor in it...thank goodness. The truly scary part of that gift is she promised to use it!

Another fun and odd gift was the jewel encrusted toilet plunger for the woman who has everything. It was a plunger worthy of any throne!

To keep the challenge in this gift exchange the hostess always provides a few really pretty and nice gifts to make the re-gift part of the game even more exciting. Matching up the correct game player with the exact gift that will make them laugh and/ or get *stingy* is what will make this a night of laughter and revenge. The rules are simple. After you have chosen one gift and revealed what it is to everyone, you will now draw a number to "take away" a gift from another guest and exchange it with what you have. Strategy is very, very important and when you have a few older Southern ladies trying to out-do each other it definitely will provide you with a fun time and **Southern Comfort** watching them turn back the clock and become kids again and naughty kids at that!

"You know I had that pretty little vase first and it will look lovely on my dining room table. I do not need or want that ugly plunger with fake jewels that you have. I have never needed to plunge my toilet and do not intend to start now. Pick on somebody else!"

Southern Comfort...
Saying Goodbye

In the past few months I have seen the newest "sweet phrase" advertised on almost every catalogue cover. It is a reminder for you to kiss you child goodnight. I honestly can't imagine putting my child or now my grandchild to bed without at least one goodnight kiss and in my case as many kisses as I could get before they said stop. How many of you have "stolen" the sweet sugar off the back of a baby's neck? I even do it to babies that are technically not related to me! That is what we in the South refer to as the "sweet sugar" even if the young one smells to high heaven from needing a diaper change.

The good night ritual with my sons also included at least one bed time story and the book for that night was read and read and read again if it was a difficult night to get still and let the sleepy time begin. I have phrases of several books storied in my memory bank from the repeated readings to my sons.

Today I have my wonderful granddaughter and she really likes to have Savannah and Molly (her loving 4 legged companion) stories more than she wants me to read from a book. Once I can finally get the wiggles out of her and keep her still for 5 minutes the story will do the rest and send her to dreamland. If she really wants to make the bedtime ritual last a few extra minutes she will tell me *"more, more"* when she is giving and receiving her night-time kisses. Who can resist a *"more, more"* when it involves hugs and kisses? Not me that's for sure!

As a teenager I traveled back and forth from our home in Kentucky to my grandparent's home in Arkansas. I always cried when I told my parents good bye and then when the visit was over I would cry when I had to give my grandparents "bye sugar". I usually can hold my feelings inside but for some reason the good bye ritual will bring me to tears almost every time. I cry now when it is time to leave Savannah even though she insists that she is fine and waves Good Bye to me.

As you can see from my multiple last names my degree of success in the marriage department has not been 100%. In my own defense I will say that marriage number one produced my oldest son so I always consider that marriage a success even if it did only last a few short years. My marriage that gave me my other wonderful son lasted 17 years and ended as painfully as any Good Bye that I have experienced except for the Good Bye associated with the death of my next husband. The good Lord decided that He needed him to come home to Him even though it meant me saying "Good bye" to a wonderful and loving husband. The night that I left to go to a fast food restaurant to bring back "non hospital" food so that he could have something good to eat and I kissed him and told him " good bye and behave yourself until I get back" was the night he left me within an hour of my leaving him and those would be the last words that I ever speak to him. Please always remember to say the words Good Bye and I love you and take care of yourself when you have the opportunity. Wishing you had said a sweet farewell to a loved one after it is too late will bring you nothing but pain and regret. I looked up the meaning of the phrase Good Bye and it said: the blending of the words Good Blessing to Ye resulted in the shortened version we use as Good Bye.

In the South we wear our affection for our loved

ones and friends right out in the open for everyone to see. We are affectionate, huggers and kiss on the cheek people, and not embarrassed by any of it. I hug people every single day...it is just part of who I *am.*

Handshakes are nice but they also give you the opportunity to bring that person in closer and follow that handshake with a hug and a pat on the back.

We show our enjoyment of being with that other person in our actions and words of greeting. Asking someone: "Well, sweetheart, how are you doing?" is not being

out-of-line here in the South. We use these simple endearments to show that we are connected to them thru our genuine concern for them. Nothing evil, sexist, lustful...or degrading is meant by these sweet words. They are simply that...*sweet words.* They sure are a big improvement over some of the hateful, sexist phrases that I continue to hear when I am unlucky enough to park next to a car that has nasty words blaring out of it via a radio station or their newest CD.

My granddaughter has a few days when she wakes up grumpy from her nap or

the-first-thing-in-the-morning-open-your-eyes part of her day. To resolve this *grumpy mood* and make her spirits bright I made up a song just for her. You can sing it to any tune and it is simply this: "It's a great day to be Savannah, OHHHHHHHHH...it's a great day to be Savannah." Sing it a few times and clap your hands and be her silly Joy Joyce and the smiles come and her world is "all right again". She needs all of her hellos to be just as important as her goodnights and good byes.

In New Orleans the tradition to have a glad parade when someone goes to the Lord makes me feel good inside. It is a wonderful way to honor the person and say our good bye with style. The tradition of having a "wake" is also a beautiful and exuberant farewell. In the South the after the funeral come by the house visit time usually provides us with a chance to remember all of the good things that we want to share with others and provides a time for smiles and even laughter. Being in the South, the North or even the South Pole does not change how you feel when a loved one is taken way too young. I delivered a stillborn son years ago and not having him to love and parent still makes my heart ache. I could have been living on the moon and the pain would have been just as painful. Sometimes saying the words good bye does not actually end the Good Bye process. It took me years to stop thinking of him every time I saw a mother with a new son.

My granddaughter already understands the ritual of leaving one person and going to another because she goes to her wonderful baby sitter every morning when her mother goes to work. Miss Margaret always welcomes her with open arms and plenty of love so when Savannah tells her mother "Good Bye" she knows that her Nonie will be there and take over and say Hello. One time she and her mom were visiting relatives and it was time to go home so that she could have her afternoon nap. She told her mom "Good Bye, I stay here, I fine, momma." She gave her momma some sweet sugar and waved Good Bye. She ended up staying with her Aunt Janet and took her nap and of course she was "just fine". Aunt Janet had promised a trip to get French fries if she took her nap and since her Aunt Janet kept her promise she truly was "fine".

The reason for sharing all of this with you is simple. When you see a Southerner hugging another person, calling them Sugar Babe, telling them how glad that they are to see them, just know that this ritual of greeting is repeated over and over again daily in almost every Southern home. We are an affectionate part of society and the open

expression of our feelings is just taken for granted.
A Southern hug brings us **Southern Comfort!**

*"Now you just get yourself right on over here. I
don't care if you are a grown man. I am your momma
and I want a big hug and a kiss on the cheek before
you leave.*

*I know that I raised you better...now get on over
here, son!"*

Southern Comfort...
The Weeping Willow

Discipline has always been at the top of the list of duties for mommas. We know the minute that our baby is placed in our arms that with love also comes duty and we are required to raise this child with love and to teach them to have respect and discipline.

My mother's childhood story on discipline for her generation has been told so many times that nobody questions her about the validity of it. Her story is about how her mother would make her go pick the switch off of the weeping willow tree that would be used to "spank" her. She swears that is why the tree is called the *weeping* willow tree.

I never heard any of these spanking stories from my grandmother Emma, so I am not sure how much of the *weeping* willow part is actually true.

I think the hickory switch is the Kentucky version of the weeping willow switch in the Deep South. I never used either one on my sons and usually the punishment was a time out followed by the lecture from me that was followed by the "I'm sorry momma and why I am sorry speech" from the little one. Dennis the Menace is not the only child who has a time out corner. Just make sure that corner doesn't include the TV or you have just wasted your time and if you send them to their room for a time out make sure the electricity to that room is turned off and anything with a battery is removed including cell phones. A corner in the kitchen is usually an effective place to make them sit. Nothing interesting or electric in there that they want to explore and it may even work out later that they noticed something needed cleaning...probably not, but who knows?

How many times did you hear "if you are going to cry, I will give you something to cry about" while you were growing up? I know that I heard it more than once and it is still a phrase available for use with the kids of this generation.

My son will tell my granddaughter to go just go ahead and get her bottom lip stuck out because she is not going to like what he is about to tell her...as in...the answer is NO...end of discussion. With that being said, how many times did you hear "what part of NO did you not understand??? and the phrase "stop asking because the answer is still "NO"?? ***But pleaseee*** didn't work too well with my parents, how about yours? Saying "NO" isn't always the easiest answer but it is the right answer. I know that there were times, many times, when it would have been so much easier to just give in and say "yes"...but I am not sure that easy is in the parenting book in the discipline section or at least not in the version that I had. What am I thinking??? Babies don't come with a book, a new owner's manual, operating guide or even a maintenance schedule. Parenting is a *learn as you go* skill, do your best and pray.

I know from first hand experience that from the time a girl starts her quest for total independence the tug-of-war to gain total control between mother and daughter has officially begun. Southern girls are brought up from day one to love and respect and obey their daddies. Talking back just is not something you do to your daddy...end of discussion. And you had better not "sass" your mother while he's listening either...trust me on that one. Daddy is here to protect his family and he also expects his little girl to protect him from the need to discipline his little darling. Never give him a reason to be "upset" with you unless it absolutely can't be avoided.

Momma is a different story. There is just

something about the female that makes her feel like she has to be the one in control so the skirmish has begun. I am not saying that the little girl doesn't love her momma...she does...but she also has to exert her independence as soon as she can. When that little girl needs her momma she expects her momma to forget all of the squabbles and be right there by her side and that is exactly what her momma does and will move heaven and earth to protect her daughter.

I always had a wonderful relationship with my grandmother Emma and I have a loving and respectful one with my mother. I do not know if it was the age difference, the fact that my grandmother had mellowed with age, or exactly what it was that made us kindred spirits. We had a special bond from the very beginning that I have never experienced with my mother. I can see that bond between my granddaughter and myself when she runs to her Joy Joyce because she is "in trouble" with her mother. It is impossible for me to stay neutral and not take her side unless she has done something so bad that even Joy Joyce is upset with her. Yes, the tolerance level is higher as a grandmother than it is as a mother. We want only the best for our grandchild but we are not the "enforcers" so that pressure is on the mother, thank goodness. I really prefer the spoiling part to the enforcing part.

My sister-in-law, Linda, and her mother have a tug-of-war relationship that at times can become an episode of "what's wrong with momma?" The two of them together make quite a pair and are very entertaining...believe me. They traveled to Alaska on a cruise with us a few years ago and those 2 staying in a small cabin together for 7 days was worth the price of the ticket. They would do whatever is necessary to protect the other one if someone was being unkind to them so their relationship is as strong as any mother/ daughter relationship can be but I swear they were Lucy and Ethel by the 2nd day of the cruise. We were never sure which one was going to "out do" the other one. The game is on the minute they get together and everything is always done with a sense of humor (sometimes a little wicked sense of humor) but definitely worth watching. Never a dull moment when those two travel with you!

As my mother reaches her older years the roles are starting to reverse and I am becoming the mother to her. Disciplining my own mother is a little tricky. It is almost like having an 80-year-old teenager when she decides she will do something that we both know she shouldn't do. She will be the first to admit that she has always been strong willed

(that would be stubborn to the rest of us) so getting her to change her mind is not an easy task. I am learning the tricks on how to get her to do what I want her to do so she won't do something that she shouldn't but since she also has many years of experience on how to get around me I'm not very successful. When she stays in Florida with my son he will call and tell me that she has just out-witted him again. Both of us agree that she is very, very good at getting around us when she wants to! Peanut butter and a bag of marshmallows in her bedroom...now does that sound like something a diabetic should have to eat? I just shake my head...shrug my shoulders...and leave her alone. As she says at her age she should be allowed to have some fun so if eating a marshmallow with peanut butter on it brings her **Southern Comfort** I will just keep buying them for her and hope that I never learn to like that snack, too!

Discipline between father and son is usually a little more solid and defined than it is between mother and daughter. The dad can read his young son from the time he starts to walk and see his past in that little one. That makes dad start to worry from that point on to the day he sees his little boy as a man. For whatever reason, the dad's in the South take the discipline responsibility very, very seriously when raising their sons. The phrase "make me proud" is taken to heart and enforced.

The dad may not remember what happened yesterday but he has total recall of how his mind worked when he was the same age as his young son. The day that young man turns thirteen his daddy's mind and memory will become a wide screen, clear as a bell, constantly running DVD of his own youth so he is always aware of what his son is probably thinking and is prepared to take action. The young one does not stand a chance!

His daddy has already been there and done that, got caught by his dad, and remembers the appropriate punishment. This of course does not stop the young one from trying and in some cases he may have learned a few tricks from his dad that improves his chances of success.

Watching your son or daughter blossom, grow and mature, into loving and considerate adults gives each and every parent profound **Southern Comfort**. It is the parent's reward for all of the love and sleepless nights that good parenting requires.

"*Now why is that I think you boys are up to something that we are all going to regret?*"

"*Daddy, we aren't up to anything...I swear.*"

"*Well, let's just keep it that way and all of you come on home with me now and we'll watch the game on TV...together.*"

Southern Comfort...
Past/Present/Future

The past is the core from which we grow. It is the root system that allows us to enjoy everything from our ancestors and to add our own "little twist" on this generation. It shapes us from the time we are just a twinkle in our daddy's eye. Before we heard the word genetics everyone knew who your grandparents and great grandparents were. I've seen the "look" jump a generation and then show up on the next and as we say in the South...he is the *"spittin image"* of his ancestor. That connection to the past always gives comfort to the family. I do not know if it turns back the clock but it definitely gives you a glimpse of what the older generation looked like in their youth.

The present is just that...a present. We are never promised another tomorrow. We wake up and it is a brand new day and it is another gift to explore. The best that we can do is make it the very best day we possibly can so when it is in the past we can be proud of how we lived that day. I tell myself every single day when I wake up...this is the youngest I will ever be, the clock does not go backwards even with the best plastic surgeon. I hope that I do not run out of life before I run out of projects. I always have more irons in the fire than I should but life is never boring.

The *future* is waiting for all of us. How many days are left in our future only the good Lord knows. You can expect to live to be 100 and hope that you do. If you do not, just make sure that when you lay your head down for the last time you can smile and remember all of the wonderful things you enjoyed while you were here. Everything that you have accomplished, every person that you have befriended, every child and grandchild you loved, that is your legacy that you leave. If you raised a couple of rascals or you raised 2 doctors it really will not matter in the big scheme of things. What does matter is that your 2 rascal doctors live by the **Southern Comfort** code. That means they share their hearts with their family and friends and make sure the next generation feels comfort in knowing them. This sharing from the heart means they are passing on the love from your heart to the next generation and to the generation after that. **This is true Southern Comfort**.

I have given you my stories to illustrate what **Southern Comfort** means to me. There are many states that make up what we fondly refer to as "The South". I have shared with you what I know from my years as a Southerner in my little part of the South. Each state in the South has its' own little twist on the Kings English. When you listen to a conversation in Tennessee English and then listen to a conversation in Alabama English you can tell that they are from two separate areas of the South. I grew up in a town located on the banks of the Mighty Muddy Mississippi River and we drove 10 minutes into Memphis at least twice a month. Memphis is a wonderful town to explore and visit. I have visited Jackson and Nashville and highly recommend both of them for their great Southern hospitality and mighty good food. I have visited Birmingham, Atlanta, Chattanooga, Louisville, Frankfort, Lexington, Bowling Green, Tupelo, Tunica, Charlotte, Gatlinburg, several small towns in Louisiana (but never New Orleans), Raleigh and almost all of the towns and cities in Arkansas. A group of us Arkansans stayed with friends in

Virginia and we visited several cities in that state years ago to show our teenagers that part of the South. It is lovely and unlike anything we have in the Delta.

I can tell you that all of the States of The South have some basic links that connect us as "The South". Most of us share a love of good sipping whiskey, enjoy seeing a spirited horse run down the race track or just gallop in the pasture, show respect to our elders and protect our children and remember to honor our parents even when they are elderly and need our care. Southern gentlemen can always be counted on to protect Southern ladies. Southern women are sweet, strong, temper-mental, fiery, intelligent, and flirtatious. Most Southern Belles can fire a gun as good as any man, drive a car or pick-up truck faster than the posted speed limit when she's "running late" and drive it like she was born with a set of keys in her hand, cook a delicious meal and serve a houseful of guests without breaking a sweat...Southern woman do not sweat, they gently perspire.

I think of **South** as my last name and I come from a big family tree. It has many, many branches but they all grow from the same set of strong and sturdy roots. It does not matter which branch your little leaf is attached to as long as you remember you are attached. I feel honored to be a woman from The South and I speak my Southern version of English with great pride. When I'm away from The South and someone politely points out that I am not "*from around here*" because of the way I talk, I always respond with pride...

"*No, Sir. I'm from parts South of here!*"

Favorite Family Recipes

I collected tried-and-true recipes from my family a few years ago to put together a family recipe book. The recipes I am sharing with you are from that recipe book...**ENJOY!**

HOMEMADE TURTLES...Christmas candy

1 small bag of Kraft Caramels (use only Kraft)
½ of 1 block of Gulf Paraffin
¼ cup Pet Milk
1 super large Hershey Chocolate Bar
2 cups pecan halves

Get your family to help you unwrap all of the caramels. Melt the caramels and pet milk in the top of a double boiler. (I have never attempted this in the microwave so I can't guarantee good results if you try it that way.) Once the caramels and milk are melted add the pecan halves. Before this has a chance to cool drop the mixture one spoonful at a time onto Reynolds wrap foil. If you spray the foil with PAM that makes it even easier to remove the candy once it cools.

Now the pan is empty, wash it and use it again to melt the paraffin and chocolate.

Use hot but not boiling water in the double boiler.

Dip the caramel /pecan mixture one piece at a time into the hot chocolate. Place the chocolate covered pieces on another sheet of Reynolds wrap foil. Once completely cool please the candy in an air-tight container.

"Rich, gooey and oh so good!"

SKILLET PINEAPPLE UPSIDE-DOWN CAKE

(My grandmother Leona's recipe) Use a cast iron skillet that measures 9 inches across.

¼ cup butter 20 oz can pineapple slices un-drained
2/3cup light brown sugar 9 maraschino cherries
2 large eggs, separated
¾ cup granulated sugar
¾ cup all purpose flour
pinch of salt
½ tsp baking powder

Melt butter in the skillet. Spread brown sugar evenly over bottom of skillet. Drain pineapple and save ¼ cup of the juice. Arrange pineapple slices in a single layer over brown sugar and place a cherry in center of each pineapple slice. Set skillet aside.

Beat egg yolks at medium speed with electric mixer, until thick and lemon colored. Gradually add granulated sugar, beating well after each addition. Heat reserved pineapple juice in a small sauce-pan over low heat. Gradually add juice to egg yolk mixture, beating until well blended. Combine all purpose flour, salt and baking powder. Add dry ingredients to the yolk mixture, beating at low speed until blended. Beat egg whites until stiff peaks form and then fold egg whites into batter. Spoon batter evenly over the pineapple slices. Bake at 325 degrees for 45 to 50 minutes. Check center with tooth-pick after 30 minutes since some ovens might be hotter than others.

"The skillet makes the difference!"

CRACKER PIE...so simple to make and you only need a few ingredients

3 egg whites
1 cup of granulated sugar
14 crushed saltine crackers (single crackers)
1 cup chopped pecans
1 tsp baking powder
1 tsp vanilla

Beat egg whites until stiff. Gradually add the cup of sugar a little at a time. Beat until the sugar/ egg white mixture has stiff peaks. Add crushed crackers, pecans, baking powder and vanilla. Pour mixture into a 9-inch un-greased pie pan.

Bake in a 325 degree oven for 25 minutes. It will light and golden brown.

"Top with Cool Whip and fresh berries...mmm, good!"

Glossary of Southern Words

Grits: a breakfast food and no, you can not order just a "grit" to see if you like it!

Cornbread: made with buttermilk and sugar and cooked in a big iron skillet.

Fried Chicken: dipped in buttermilk, then coated with seasoned flour and fried in a big iron skillet until golden brown.

Ice Tea: sweet Lipton tea with plenty of sugar and served over ice cubes.

Pecan Pie: use only the best and freshest pah-kahns and Karo Syrup when making this

Cornbread in buttermilk: Big glass of ice-cold buttermilk with a large piece of cornbread crumbled up in it & you eat it with a spoon.

Cookin on a disc blade: Southern Farmer's Wok

I'll be diddled: taken advantage of/ surprised

Mess of it: nice big portion/ bowl or pan full

Lopper Jawed: out of balance

I'm fixin' to: you arc just about to do something

Y'all: can be plural or single...you all/ everyone

Ice Box: refrigerator

Caddie Whompus: crooked

Honey, Darlin, Dear, Sweetie, Hon, Sugar, Baby: terms of endearment liberally used in the South

Fair to Middlin: cotton-grading term that means "not bad"

Month of Sundays: too many days

Tuckered out/ worn to a frazzle: very, very tired

C'mon: come on/ move it/ keep up

Fiddle Sticks: polite cussing

Daylight to plenty past dark: A farmer's normal working hours

Angel Kisses: freckles

Screen Door Tan: freckles

Farmer Tan: brown arms below shirt-sleeves, brown face and neck and sunburned ears

Whoopin: spanking

Spittin image: looks just like someone

Galavantin: up to no good/ probably getting into trouble

Miss Priss/ Prissy: female with a tendency to strut around

Uppity: female or male with their nose up in the air...puttin' on "airs"

Sweet Sugar: innocent kisses, sugar kisses from
my grandchild.

*Y'all come back now...the porch light is always on
and the welcome mat is out!*